Home is a Place Called Nowhere

She was tired of running, tired of roaming the streets. She seemed to have done nothing but run ever since she'd left Auntie Victoria's . . . All she wanted now was to go home, only she didn't know where home was.

Amina runs away from the only home she has ever known, desperate to find her mother and learn the truth about where she comes from and where her real home is. But where should she start looking? And what will happen if she is caught?

She meets up with Paul, another runaway, and together they enter the twilight world of asylum seekers, hiding from the police and from angry people who think all immigrants should be sent back home. But Amina doesn't know where home is and until she finds her mother and learns the truth, for her home will always be a place called nowhere . . .

Leon Rosselson was born in London and has been writing songs for children and adults since the 1960s. He has sung all round the world and has had two songs in the Indie singles charts. He has also written several stories for children and has been shortlisted for the Carnegie Medal. He is married, with two daughters and two grandchildren. When not writing or singing he enjoys playing football with his grandson, playing the guitar, and going on peace demonstrations. *Home is a Place Called Nowhere* is his first book for Oxford University Press.

Home is a Place Called Nowhere

Home is a Place Called Nowhere

Leon Rosselson

OXFORD
UNIVERSITY PRESS

OXFORD
UNIVERSITY PRESS

Great Clarendon Street, Oxford OX2 6DP

Oxford University Press is a department of the University of Oxford.
It furthers the University's objective of excellence in research, scholarship,
and education by publishing worldwide in

Oxford   New York

Auckland   Cape Town   Dar es Salaam   Hong Kong   Karachi
Kuala Lumpur   Madrid   Melbourne   Mexico City   Nairobi
New Delhi   Shanghai   Taipei   Toronto

With offices in

Argentina   Austria   Brazil   Chile   Czech Republic   France   Greece
Guatemala   Hungary   Italy   Japan   Poland   Portugal   Singapore
South Korea   Switzerland   Thailand   Turkey   Ukraine   Vietnam

Oxford is a registered trade mark of Oxford University Press
in the UK and in certain other countries

British Library Cataloguing in Publication Data available

ISBN 978-0-19-272586-8

5   7   9   10   8   6

Typeset by AFS Image Setters Ltd, Glasgow

Printed in Great Britain by
CPI Cox & Wyman, Reading, RG1 8EX

Paper used in the production of this book is a natural,
recyclable product made from wood grown in sustainable forests.
The manufacturing process conforms to the environmental
regulations of the country of origin.

To my grandson Michael
and for a better world

Thanks to Javad Shams; Alison Harvey of the Medical
Foundation for the Care of Victims of Torture;
Gill Boden of the Campaign to Close Campsfield;
Doris Bancroft, Nina Chohda, and the refugee children
of Salusbury Road Primary School in Brent; Robb
Johnson and the refugee children of the Alexandra
Nursery and Infants School, Hounslow.

1

'Run, Amina, run'

She could hear the waves roaring and feel the wind choking her.

And the voice in her head: 'Run, Amina, run.'

Now she was running as fast as she could. The stones were jabbing at her feet. Behind her, the angry waves lashed at the shore, launching themselves at her, threatening to drag her back and swallow her up.

And the woman's voice echoing in her head: 'Run, Amina, run.'

But though she was running, she was not moving. Their heavy breathing was in her ears. Their arms were reaching out to grab her. She was running and not moving. She couldn't breathe any more. She couldn't run any more. A giant wave rose over her and sucked her down—

Amina sat up with a start. That dream again. The same dream. Her legs ached as if she'd been running in her sleep. Where was she? The smell of dust and damp made her chest wheeze. She peered into the gloom and then reached out for the torch beside the mattress and switched it on. There was a scuttling sound. Cockroaches? Mice? She shivered. There was nothing in the room but the mattress she was lying on, the blankets that covered her and a broken chair propped against the wall. The floorboards were bare. Cobwebs hung from the ceiling and the walls were a patchwork of torn paper, paint, and graffiti. There was no light, only a bare wire hanging from the middle of the ceiling. Someone had scribbled 'Death to the invader' in large red letters on one wall.

She'd thought, when she'd climbed into the house, that it was empty. Now she wasn't so sure. There were signs that someone had been living there. The mattress and the blankets for a start. And she'd seen in the kitchen downstairs a tea-stained cup and a plate with the yellow remains of an egg on it. She'd been too tired to explore the rest of the house. She'd just climbed upstairs, found the mattress and blankets and collapsed into an exhausted sleep.

She wondered if she should get up or try to go back to sleep again. She had no watch. She didn't know what time it was. She padded over to the window and looked out. There was no moon. The sky was covered with a thick carpet of cloud. The street lamps were still on. The curfew police were probably still out there somewhere. An old man, shabbily dressed, was just turning the corner. A car drove past. A police siren blared quite close by and then faded into the distance. She felt something sharp prick her foot through her sock and hopped back to the mattress. She removed the splinter, curled up once again under the blankets, her head resting on her bag, and closed her eyes.

She didn't want to dream that dream again so she tried to fix her mind on something cheerful. She was in a field with hundreds of other children. They were all her friends and they were playing and laughing together. There were butterflies and flowers and colourful birds. The sun shone down out of a clear blue sky. Her mother was there, too, though she couldn't quite make out her face.

Suddenly she stiffened. The picture in her head dissolved. A noise downstairs made her sit up. She could hear it clearly. Somebody else was in the house. She started to put on her trainers, then hesitated. Was there time to run? The window was too high to jump from but she might be able to run downstairs and out of the door before anyone could catch her. She was a good quick runner. She had to be. But there was still the curfew. The police would be on the lookout for kids like her. And she was tired of running, tired of roaming the streets. She seemed to have done nothing but run ever since she'd left Auntie Victoria's.

It was too late now anyway. Footsteps were on the stairs. Someone was coming up to the room. Well, if she was caught, she was caught. In a way it would be a relief. All she wanted now was to go home, only she didn't know where home was. She began to sing quietly to herself a song that she'd made up. She always sang it when she was in a tight spot. It comforted her.

'There's a place that I call nowhere
It's far across the sea
There's a woman there who's singing

And she's singing songs for me
There's a place that I call nowhere
And it's where I want to be
There's a woman there who's waiting
And she's waiting there for me—'

The door creaked open and the light from a torch beamed onto her. She picked up her own torch and beamed a light back onto the intruder. It was a boy, a tall, thin boy, pale-faced, much older than her. She guessed he was about sixteen or seventeen. He had short hair. He wore jeans and a dirty white T-shirt. A silver ring dangled from one ear. He carried a bag on his shoulder.

'Jeepers creepers,' he said frowning. 'Do I know you?'

Amina said nothing but kept the torch beam directed on the boy's face.

'Turn that off,' he said and took a step towards her.

'I'll scream,' she said. 'I've got a really loud scream.'

The boy laughed.

'I've got a knife,' Amina said. 'I know how to use it.'

'You're really scaring me,' the boy said.

The beam from Amina's torch followed him as he walked round the bottom of the mattress and went to a small wall cupboard in the corner. Amina hadn't noticed that cupboard before. He took out a candle on a saucer and a box of matches, lit the candle and placed it on the floor. Then he removed the bag from his shoulder, sat on the floor with his back to the wall and switched off his torch.

'Your turn,' he said.

Amina switched off her torch. They examined each other by the flickering light of the candle.

'OK,' the boy said at last. 'Who are you and what are you doing here?'

'I didn't know anyone lived here,' Amina said.

'You're just a child,' the boy said. 'You should be at home.'

Amina said nothing.

'Don't you have a home to go to?'

Amina stared at him silently.

The boy sighed. 'We're not getting very far, are we?' he said. 'My name's Paul. Do you have a name?'

'Yes,' Amina whispered.

Still Amina was silent.

'OK,' Paul said. 'Let me guess. Cinderella? Rapunzel? Cakeface?'

In spite of herself, Amina smiled. 'Amina,' she said.

'Funny name,' the boy said. 'Are you English?'

'I don't know,' Amina mumbled.

'You don't look English,' Paul said. 'I'm English.'

'Why aren't you at home then?' Amina asked.

'Arguments,' Paul said. 'Too many arguments. Got into trouble. More arguments. Got thrown out. Came down here. Slept in the streets. Slept in doorways. Slept in the cemetery once. Spooky. Found this job in a café. Washing up. Clearing up. Rubbish job. Food's not bad though. And it's money in my pocket. No questions asked. Found this house. No one wanted it. So I made myself at home. Till I find myself something better. When I'm rich. I'm going to be rich, you know. And famous.'

'How?' Amina asked.

'Haven't decided yet,' Paul said. 'Might be a famous writer. Might get a band together. I haven't decided yet.'

'What do you play?' Amina asked.

'Guitar,' Paul said.

'I don't see a guitar,' Amina said.

'It's in the music room.'

'What music room?'

'Well, it's just a room really. Next door. With a guitar in it.'

There was a silence. Amina sat with her chin resting on her knee staring at the candle. She didn't know what to make of this boy.

'So that's me,' Paul said. 'Your turn.'

Amina shook her head.

Paul raised his eyes to the ceiling and exclaimed, 'Jeepers creepers!'

'Why do you keep saying that?' Amina asked. 'What's it mean, anyway?'

'I dunno,' Paul said. 'I just like the sound of it. I found it in a book. I do a lot of reading,' he said. 'I like reading. Look.'

He went to the cupboard door and opened it. 'See?'

Amina leaned over and peered into the cupboard. There were dusty books piled up on the shelf.

'You can borrow one if you like,' Paul said. 'Can you read?'

'Yes,' Amina said in a low voice.

'Well then,' Paul went on, 'if I let you stay, you can borrow my books. And I might let you stay, if you tell me a good story.'

'What sort of a good story?'

'Your story,' Paul said. 'If you tell me your story and if it's a good story, I might let you stay.'

Amina stared at him, examining his face

carefully, trying to decide if she could trust him or not.

He smiled at her encouragingly.

'Promise you won't tell anyone,' Amina said.

'Oh, sure. I promise.'

'You won't give me up?'

'Give you up? Who to?'

'The police. The truancy agency. Anyone.'

'Course not. What do you take me for?'

'All right,' Amina said. 'I'll tell you what I know. But I don't know everything. I don't remember everything.'

'It'd better be a good story,' Paul said.

2

'All she knew was my name'

'I don't know where to start,' Amina said.

'Begin at the beginning,' Paul said.

'There wasn't a beginning,' Amina said. 'I don't remember it. I don't know how I got here. I don't know where I came from. I don't remember anything before Auntie Victoria's. I only know what she told me.'

'So what did Auntie Victoria tell you?'

'She found me. She opened the door one morning and found me. I was fast asleep in a cardboard box she'd left on the doorstep to put old newspapers in. That's what she told me.'

'Where was this?' Paul asked.

'Dover,' Amina said.

'Never been there,' Paul said. 'Were you left there by gypsies?'

'I remember running,' Amina said. 'I do remember that. My feet were all cut and bleeding when Auntie Victoria found me. That's what she said. I dream about it sometimes. Auntie Victoria said she'd heard about a boatload of refugees landing during the night. The police had caught them and they'd been locked up. Cos they were illegal. She said I must have escaped somehow and found my way to her house. It was quite near the sea. Perhaps I was so small they didn't notice me in the dark.'

'Are you illegal then?' Paul asked.

'I suppose so. I feel like I'm illegal anyway.'

'What about your mum and dad?'

Amina shrugged. 'I think my father's dead. I think he was killed. I think he was. I don't really know. I don't remember him. Sometimes I think I remember my mother. Sometimes I think I can see her face almost. Especially when I'm asleep. Sometimes she speaks to me. She calls my name. Only she speaks in English. I don't think she spoke English to me.'

'It's a good story,' Paul said. 'I like it.'

'Auntie Vickie said she tried to find out who I belonged to. I don't think she tried very hard though. I think she wanted to keep me. She said she didn't want to ask too many questions in case the people in charge got suspicious. So I don't know what happened to my mum and the people on the boat. Perhaps they were sent away. Perhaps they're still here somewhere. I don't really know.'

'I don't understand,' Paul said. 'Weren't you old enough to talk or something?'

'Auntie Victoria said I didn't say anything for months. It was as if I'd forgotten how to speak. I just wouldn't talk. All she knew was my name.'

'How did she know that?'

'Because of this.'

Amina pulled at a gold chain around her neck to reveal at the end of it a gold disc and a key.

'My name's written here,' she said. 'Amina.'

'What about the key?' Paul asked. 'What's that for?'

'I don't know,' Amina said. 'I don't know what it's for.'

'A mystery,' Paul said.

'There's another word on it as well. Look.'

She showed the gold disc to Paul. He tried to read it by the light of the candle.

'I can't read it properly,' he said. 'What's it say?'

'It says Qalunya.'

'Qalunya. Funny word. What's it mean?'

'Dunno. Might be a magic word. Might be my second name.'

'Another mystery,' Paul said. 'It's like in a book.'

'After a time, I started speaking English words,' Amina went on. 'The other language has gone now. I've forgotten it.'

'Did Auntie Vickie adopt you?' Paul asked.

'No. She just kept me. She should have adopted me really. I might not have been illegal then. But she didn't. She said it was too complicated. She was frightened of losing me. She really loved me. She called me her little brown baby. She made up some story about her sister dying and leaving me an orphan so she was looking after me. She didn't want anyone to know I might be one of the refugees. They hate refugees in that place. They call them names.'

There was a silence. Amina fingered her gold chain nervously. Paul waited for her to continue.

'I'm tired,' Amina said. 'Is it morning yet?'

'No,' Paul said. 'Nowhere near. Finish your story then you can go back to sleep.'

'There's not much more to tell. Auntie

Vickie looked after me. She sent me to school. She was good to me. She had three children of her own. She didn't have a husband. I don't know what happened to him. Her children were older than me. Cleo and Lawrence. I got on well with them. Mostly. And James. He was the oldest. He hated me. He was jealous because Auntie Victoria loved me best. It's all his fault.'

'What is?'

'Everything.'

'Explain,' Paul said.

'He used to say things about me at school. He used to wait at the school gate and tell the other children not to be friends with me. He used to call me names. Dirty refugee. Things like that. He said I didn't belong there and I'd get found out one day. He said he'd read about refugees in the papers and we were all criminals and scroungers. Some of the children picked on me. Tried to bully me.'

'Why?' Paul asked.

'Cos I looked different, I suppose. Cos I didn't belong. But I got fed up with their name-calling and pushing me and throwing things at me. So I found a way to stop them.'

'How?'

'Singing.'

'Singing?' Paul raised his eyebrows in disbelief. 'What good did that do?'

'I told you. It stopped them. I can sing really loudly when I want. So when they picked on me, I started singing at them in my loudest voice. I made up a special song to sing. A really fierce song. It was like magic. They backed off. They thought I was weird. In the end, they left me alone.'

'I wish I'd thought of that when I got picked on,' Paul said. 'But you still haven't told me why you're here.'

'It was all James's fault. Like I said. He hated me. We used to have terrible arguments. Then one Saturday we had a fight. Auntie Vickie was out shopping with Cleo and Lawrence. I was making myself some toast in the kitchen. James started on me, teasing me and calling me stupid names. I just ignored him but he wouldn't stop. He just went on shouting at me and calling me horrible names. I started singing cos that's what I do when I'm upset. I was only singing to myself, pretending that I wasn't listening to him. That made him really angry. He lost his temper and started attacking me and hitting me and lashing out at me. So I grabbed a knife from the table and—'

'What?' asked Paul.

'Stabbed him.'

'Jeepers creepers!' Paul said, genuinely shocked. 'What happened then?'

'I'm tired,' Amina said.

'Did he die? He didn't die, did he?'

'Course not. It was only in the arm. It was just a cut but there was a lot of blood. I didn't really mean it. I just wanted to stop him hitting me.'

Paul waited for her to continue but she shook her head. 'I can't talk any more,' she said.

The candle had burned low by this time. Paul put his hand palms down over the flickering flame as if to warm them. 'It's a good story,' he said. 'But I want to know the ending.'

'I'll tell you tomorrow,' Amina said.

'Well, OK,' Paul said doubtfully. 'But you should be at home, you know. You're just a child. You should go back to your Auntie Victoria.'

'I can't,' Amina said.

'It'd be all right,' Paul said. 'I'm sure it would. You wouldn't get into trouble or anything.'

'I don't belong there,' Amina said. 'It's not my home. Auntie Vickie's been good to me and everything but I always knew it wasn't my home. And I never want to see James again.'

'How are you going to live?' Paul asked. 'What do you want to do?'

'I want to find my mother. I want to find out who I am.'

The candle spluttered, the flame burned lower and lower and then died. A wisp of smoke rose from the lump of melted wax in the saucer.

'How are you going to do that?'

Amina shrugged. 'There must be a way. Somebody must know.'

Paul yawned. 'Well,' he said, 'we'll talk about it in the morning. You go back to sleep.'

'What about you?' Amina said. 'I've taken your bed.'

'I'm going to play the guitar a bit,' Paul said. 'I don't sleep much at night anyway. Don't worry. I'll be all right.'

He stood up, waved a hand and disappeared out of the door. Amina lay back under the blankets. She was more tired than she'd ever been. But she felt comforted to know that she wasn't alone in the house. The boy was about the same age as James but he wasn't at all like James. Maybe he could be a friend. Maybe.

The sound of Paul's guitar filtered through the wall. He was singing, too, in a strange strangled voice. Amina smiled to herself. He'll never get rich that way, she thought. She pulled the blankets over her head and fell asleep.

She opened her eyes and saw that it was day. It took her a little while to recognize the room and remember why she was there. No sound came from the room next door. The boy must have fallen asleep. She put on her trainers and went to look out of the window. The sky was still covered by a thick layer of white cloud. It was summer but where was the sun? An empty ache in her stomach reminded her that she was hungry. Perhaps there'd be something to eat in the kitchen. It was time to explore the house.

Ten minutes later she was back. She'd found some stale bread and mouldy cheese in the kitchen. There was no fridge and no stove. Just a primus. There was one plate (dirty), one cup (stained and chipped), and one frying pan (unwashed). Nothing else. In the bathroom, there was a toilet which flushed, for which she was grateful, and a sink with taps that ran cold water so that, at least, she could wash her hands and face and dry them on the pile of green paper towels. But there was no furniture anywhere, no comforts of any sort. If this was to be her home, it wasn't very welcoming. Perhaps Paul was right. She ought to go back to Auntie Vickie's. Auntie Vickie would be worried to death wondering where she'd got to. But the thought of facing James, of explaining why she'd stabbed him, gave her a sick feeling in the pit of her stomach.

A tear trickled down her cheek. She wiped it away and went to see if Paul was awake. The door creaked as she pushed it open. Paul was sprawled in a corner of the room hugging his guitar to his chest. She wondered how he could have slept like that. The only other object in the room was a clock on the mantelpiece. As she stood there wondering whether to wake him or not, he opened his eyes, sat up, yawned and strummed a loud chord on the guitar.

'Hey!' he said. 'You woke me up.'

'I'm hungry,' Amina said.

'I know who you are,' Paul said. 'You ran away from Auntie Victoria and want to find your mother. Right? Why are you up so early?'

'I'm hungry,' Amina said again. 'There's no proper food in the house.'

'OK,' Paul said dragging himself to his feet. 'We'll go and have breakfast at the Crescent Moon—that's the café where I work.'

'It's too dangerous,' Amina said. 'They'll want to know who I am.'

'I'll say you're my long-lost sister,' Paul said.

'I don't look anything like you,' Amina protested.

'They won't care. There's all sorts go to that café. Foreigners. All sorts of dodgy characters. They won't give you away. Come on. And while we're having breakfast, we'll make a plan of action. OK?'

'OK,' Amina said.

'You'll have to go out through the window,' Paul said. 'The door doesn't open.'

As Amina went through the door of the Crescent Moon café, she was met by a blast of hot air and the smell of frying. She felt slightly sick. Most of the customers seemed to be men eating fried eggs. A young dark-haired woman carrying plates of eggs and toast and baked beans greeted Paul and pointed to a table in the corner.

'That's Leyla,' Paul said. 'She's one of your refugees.'

'Where's she from?' Amina asked.

Paul hesitated. 'I've forgotten,' he said. 'Some foreign country I've never heard of.'

Paul ordered bacon on toast and tea and Amina asked for baked beans on toast and a cup of hot chocolate. When Paul offered her a piece of his bacon, she shook her head.

'I don't eat meat,' she said. 'I don't eat animals.'

Paul looked surprised. 'Why not?'

'I like animals,' she said. 'I don't like to think of eating them.'

Paul grinned. 'I like animals, too,' he said. 'Especially sliced up and fried on toast.'

Amina screwed up her face in disgust.

By the time they'd finished eating, most of the other customers had left. There were just four men at one table talking loudly in a language Amina didn't understand. Leyla came over and sat down with them.

'I don't know why I stay here,' she said. 'It's a mad place. From six o'clock in the morning I've been serving. No sitting down, not once.'

'You should try washing up at night like me,' Paul said. 'That's worse.'

'And what are you doing with this child, Paul?' Leyla asked.

'This is Amina,' Paul said. 'My long-lost sister.'

'No,' Leyla said smiling. 'But *my* long-lost sister she could be.'

'Maybe she is,' Paul said.

'Where are you from, Amina?' Leyla asked.

'Nowhere,' Amina said.

'Nowhere,' Leyla repeated. 'I also am from nowhere.'

Paul looked puzzled. 'I thought you said you were from that country I've forgotten with the long name.'

'Kurdistan,' Leyla said.

'That's the one,' Paul said.

'It is a name without a country,' Leyla said. 'It is a country yet to be born. It is a nowhere place.'

'I don't understand,' Paul said.

Leyla ignored him. 'And what are you doing here, little sister, with this English boy?'

Amina didn't reply.

'How old are you?'

'I don't know,' Amina said.

'It's a long story,' Paul interrupted. 'She's lost her mother. I'm going to help her find her.'

Before Leyla could ask any more questions, a man burst through the door and shouted something. Paul and Amina looked at each other. What was he saying? The four men still sitting in the café jumped to their feet, nearly overturning the table. All five men then charged under the serving counter and disappeared out the back. The large woman sitting behind the cash register made no effort to stop them. Leyla stood up and exclaimed something which sounded to Amina like a curse.

'What's going on?' Paul asked.

'A raid,' Leyla said. 'They're looking for illegals.'

'What shall we do?' cried Amina. 'I don't want to be caught.'

'Go the way the men went,' Leyla ordered. 'There's a way out through the kitchen.'

Amina hesitated and looked over at the fat woman still sitting impassively behind the cash register. 'We haven't paid,' she said.

'You pay next time,' Leyla replied. 'Mrs Onen understands. She is a good woman. Quick.'

But it was too late. Two men marched into the café. They were wearing identical dark blue suits and, so it seemed to Amina, menacing expressions. Her body tensed. She prepared herself to run.

3

'Catching illegals. That's our job.'

'Who are they?' Amina asked.

Leyla put her hand on her shoulder and whispered, 'They're from immigration. Don't worry. I will talk to them. You will be my sister. If they talk to you, you do not speak English. Be calm.'

Amina and Paul watched as one of the men went to talk to Mrs Onen. He had a heavy red face and thick lips. The other man sat Leyla at a table and began to question her. They could see that she was becoming more and more angry. He seemed to be writing down everything she said in a notebook.

'Remember,' Paul whispered, 'you don't speak English.'

The man who'd been talking to Mrs Onen glanced round at them and then walked over and said brusquely, 'Well? What are you doing here?'

Paul looked at him and grinned. 'Who's asking?' he said.

The man's red face grew even redder. 'Any more cheek from you, sonny, and you're in trouble.'

'Are you the police?' Paul asked.

The man took something from his pocket and held it out for Paul to read. It was a warrant card.

'Immigration Officer,' Paul said aloud.

'That's right, sonny,' the man said. 'We're looking for illegals. People who shouldn't be here. Living here without permission.'

'What do you do when you find them?' Paul asked.

'Send them packing,' Redface said. 'Back where they came from. And how about you, sonny? Are you one of them?'

'I just came in for breakfast,' Paul said. 'I'm English.'

'So you say,' the man said. 'Maybe you're lying. Maybe we should take you in for questioning. Maybe you know some illegals and you're not telling us.'

'No,' Paul said nervously.

'How old are you?'

'Seventeen,' Paul said.

'Name?'

'Yes,' Paul said.

'What's your name, sonny?'

'Paul. Paul Wilson.'

'Proof of identity?'

'What?'

'Proof of identity. Birth certificate? Driving licence? Passport? Credit card?'

Paul shook his head.

'You don't exist then, sonny, do you? You're a nobody, aren't you? Where do you live? In the streets? A beggar, are you? Are you one of those beggars? Come on, own up. You're one of those beggars, one of those pathetic beggars in the streets asking for money. That's right, isn't it? Asking for money. Go on, say it. Spare any change, mister?'

Paul's pale face turned even whiter. 'No, I'm not.'

'A thief, then. You're a thief, aren't you, sonny?'

'No,' Paul said indignantly. 'I work.'

'Work? Don't give me that. Your sort don't work.' Then turning suddenly to Amina, he bent over and, putting his red face close to hers, he almost shouted: 'What about you, little miss? What are you doing here?'

Amina saw the black hairs protruding from his nostrils and felt his hot sour breath smelling of tobacco on her face. She turned away. In her head, a song formed itself.

'She doesn't speak English,' Paul said. 'She's that girl's sister.'

'Doesn't speak English? Doesn't speak English? Why doesn't she speak English?'

'Don't know,' Paul said. 'I think she's a bit—' He tapped his forehead. 'You know.'

Before the man could say anything more, the other man who'd been questioning Leyla called him over. Amina felt angry and humiliated. If that man came back again, she didn't think she'd be able to stop herself from answering him back. She'd show him she could speak English. To her relief, she saw that, after a brief conversation, both men were making for the door. As they left, the man who'd been questioning them wagged his finger at Paul and said, 'You watch it, sonny. I know your sort.'

There was a moment's silence. Mrs Onen sighed, got up from her chair behind the cash register, and disappeared into the kitchen. Leyla was holding her head in her hands and staring at the table.

Paul breathed an audible sigh of relief. 'Jeepers creepers!' he said. 'What a monster! I thought he was going to beat me up.'

Amina banged her fist on the table, still trembling with fear and fury. 'Why did you say I was daft?' she burst out. 'I'm not daft. You're daft. I can speak English better than that man anyway.'

'OK. OK.' Paul held up a hand as if to ward off her attack. 'I'm sorry. I didn't know what else to say.'

Leyla came back and sat down. Amina could see she was seething with anger.

'What did he want?' Paul asked.

'Another interrogation,' she said. 'Like when I come to this country. They want to know everything and then they don't believe what I tell them. They treat me like a criminal. I am here nearly two years. I am still waiting to see if I am allowed to stay as a refugee. I have done nothing wrong. But they treat me like a criminal. They have no respect.'

'They questioned me, too,' Paul said.

'They are not interested in you,' Leyla said. 'They are just having fun with you. They are interested only in illegals. Catching illegals.'

'It's a rotten job,' Paul said. 'But I suppose somebody has to do it.'

'Why?' Leyla said. 'You come to my country with nothing, you are welcome. We share. That is how we are taught. A stranger in your house is an honoured guest. Here, you are rich. You have everything and you want to give nothing. When I read the bad things they say about us, it is like a stone hurled at my heart. You treat us like animals. You have no respect.'

'I'm not rich,' Paul said. 'And I do respect you.'

Leyla smiled. 'Thank you,' she said. 'Of course, I don't mean everyone.'

'What did you tell them about me?' Amina asked.

'He wanted to know everything,' Leyla said. 'Who I am, why I am here, where I am living. I tell him we live five of us in a dirty hotel. Five in one room. My family. Share a kitchen. Queue for the bathroom. Five of us. He will go and check that what I am telling him is true. I tell him you are my sister. He asks why you are not at school. I say it is a Kurdish holiday today. What does he know? He knows nothing. Stupid man!'

'They'll catch me in the end, though, won't they?' Amina said tearfully. 'What will they do to me? Where will they send me? I don't belong here. I don't belong anywhere.'

'You should go back,' Paul said. 'That's what I think.'

'Can I help?' Leyla said. 'Is there something I can do?'

'Tell her, Amina,' Paul said. 'You can trust Leyla.'

So Amina explained to Leyla how she'd been found and brought up by Aunt Victoria. She showed her the gold disc with her name on.

'What's the key?' Leyla asked.

'I don't know,' Amina said.

'There's another word on there,' Paul said. 'After her name.'

'So there is,' Leyla said. She screwed up her eyes and peered at it. 'Qalunya. What's Qalunya?'

'Don't know,' Amina said.

'Mysterious, isn't it?' Paul said.

'Why did you run away from Aunt Victoria?' Leyla asked.

Amina told her about the fight with James and the stabbing.

'I didn't mean it,' Amina said.

Leyla smiled at her. 'I understand,' she said. 'I have done worse things.'

'You never told me what happened after that,' Paul said.

'It was awful,' Amina said. 'I ran upstairs to the room I share with Cleo. James chased after me but I locked the door. He yelled at me that he was going to tell the police that I was a murderer and I was illegal and they'd lock me up. In the end, he went away. I stayed in my room all day. I wouldn't come out. When Auntie Victoria came back, she tried to get me to unlock the door but I wouldn't. She said I wouldn't get into trouble or anything. She talked to me for ages. I didn't answer. I was lying on my bed crying and pretending I was somewhere else. I just wanted to be somewhere else. She left me alone in the end. I just lay there all day. I could hear lots of noise from downstairs. People coming and going. Doors banging. Then I fell asleep. When I woke up, it was dark. I thought I'd better come out and see what was happening. I wanted something to eat as well. I was ravenous. I unlocked the door and tiptoed onto the landing. That's when I heard them talking.'

'Who?' Paul asked.

'The police. James. Auntie Victoria. James must have gone to the police. I didn't think he really would. I couldn't hear what they were saying but I knew they were talking about me. I heard my name. That's when I decided. I had to leave. I couldn't stay there any more. It wasn't my home any more. They were going to take me away. I put some stuff in a bag, things I thought I might need, all the pocket money I'd saved at Auntie Vickie's, and I climbed out of the window.'

'I thought you said your room was upstairs,' Paul said.

'Yes. But there's a flat roof outside the window. From there I could reach a branch of the apple tree in the garden. I climbed onto the branch. I was terrified it was going to break. I sat on the branch and wriggled my way along till I reached the trunk. It was easy to climb down from there. I went out through the side entrance into the street. Nobody saw me. It was dark.'

'When was this?' Paul asked.

'Saturday. Three days ago.'

'But how did you come to London?' Leyla asked.

'When I left the house,' Amina said, 'I didn't know what to do. I just knew I had to get away. And I knew if the police or anyone found me on the streets, I'd be in trouble. You're not allowed on the streets at night by yourself if you're my age. And there were lots of police about. Because of the illegals. They're always looking for people who aren't supposed to be there.'

'Yes,' Leyla said. 'I know.'

'So I thought I'd better keep out of the way till it was day. Just down the road from Auntie Victoria's there was a van parked. The back was covered with tarpaulin. It was full of bricks. I squeezed under the tarpaulin and curled up in a corner. It was really dirty and uncomfortable. My stomach was rumbling cos I was so hungry. I almost decided to give up and go back. Then I heard police sirens and people running in the streets and lots of commotion. I thought they'd probably discovered I'd gone and were looking for me. I was frightened. I didn't know what they'd do if they found me. But they didn't look in the van. I lay awake for hours. In the end, I must have fallen asleep because the next thing I knew it was daylight and the van was bumping along somewhere. I didn't know where we were going. I was aching all over. After a time, the van stopped and the cover was taken off and I saw this big man with a bald head. His mouth dropped open when he saw me. Before he could do anything, I was off the van and running down the street as fast as I could. He didn't chase me. He wouldn't have caught me anyway. I'm a good runner.'

'So that's how you got to London,' Paul said.

'I didn't know where I was at first. I spent the day walking around the streets and in and out of shops. Whenever I saw anyone looking at me, I ran. I did a lot of running that day. I bought myself chips and a veggieburger. I went to a supermarket and bought some more stuff. I found a station and went all over London on a tube train. It was fun in a way. I felt free. Nobody to tell me anything. It was like an adventure. I ended up in a park. It had a children's playground with a sort of tree house in it. That's where I spent the night. In the tree house. I didn't sleep much. I just sat there listening to the scary night noises. Lucky it's summer so I wasn't cold. The next day was Monday. I'd planned what I was going to do. I thought if people see me in the streets, they'll want to know why I'm not at school. So, early in the morning, I took the tube to Kensington because I'd seen an advertisement that said all the museums were there. I spent the day in the Science Museum. There were lots of children so nobody noticed me. In the evening, I thought I'd go to the park and the tree house but as I was walking there I saw two policemen looking at me so I ran. I ran as fast as I could. Then I didn't know where I was. I saw these empty houses but all the windows were boarded up so I couldn't get in. Until I found Paul's house. I opened the back window and climbed in.'

'I did that,' Paul said. 'I got the window open.'

'I didn't know anyone lived there,' Amina said.

'I thought you were a ghost at first,' Paul said. 'Then when I saw you were just a child, I couldn't believe it.'

Amina frowned. She wished Paul wouldn't keep calling her a child. 'Paul thinks I should go back,' she said. 'But I'm not going to. I've got to find my mother . . .'

'But how will you live?' Paul said. 'You're only a child. Children your age should be safe at home.'

'In my country,' Leyla said, 'children her age walk hundreds of kilometres, cross borders, face guns and bombs and soldiers. Maybe they have seen their fathers killed, their mothers killed. Yes, children her age.'

'I'm not going back,' Amina said.

'I think she will not be happy until she knows who she is and where she comes from,' Leyla said. 'But what about your Aunt Victoria, Amina? She will be very worried about you.'

'Yes,' Amina said. 'She will. I'll phone her. Tell her I'm all right.'

'They'll be able to trace the phone call,' Paul said knowingly. 'They'll soon find you.'

'Write a letter,' Leyla suggested. 'I'll post it in another part of London.'

Amina was reassured. 'Yes,' she said. 'And Paul said he'd help me find my mother.'

'How will he do that?' Leyla asked.

They both looked at Paul who looked at the ceiling, scratched his head, frowned and said, 'Dunno yet.'

'Before you came to this country,' Leyla asked, 'is there nothing you remember?'

'I'm not sure,' Amina said. 'Sometimes I think I remember. Sometimes I think I remember my mother. I have dreams. I see her in dreams. I hear her voice. Sometimes she sings to me. But I don't know what's real and what's dreams.'

'If you knew when you came here—' Paul began.

'I can tell you that,' Amina interrupted. 'I do know that.'

'How?' Paul asked.

'Auntie Vickie used to celebrate it like it was my birthday. She didn't know my real birthday so she made the day she found me my birthday. It was the twenty-first of July. Seven years ago.'

'That's next Saturday,' Paul said. 'You'll be seven. We should have a party.'

'Auntie Vickie thinks I'm probably eleven,' Amina said.

'There must be newspapers,' Paul said. 'If we could find newspapers of that time, we might find something.'

Amina looked at him hopefully. Maybe he *would* be able to help her find her mother. She wanted it so much but in her heart she hadn't believed it was possible. It was all so long ago, the memories of that lost time buried under the years of living with Aunt Victoria in England. But now, with Paul to help her, and maybe Leyla, she found a spark of hope.

Paul looked at her and grinned. 'Isn't it funny?' he said. 'All you want to do is find your mum and all I want to do is escape from mine. And my dad.'

'Don't they know where you are?' Amina asked. 'Don't you ever see them?'

Paul shook his head. 'They know I'm in London,' he said. 'But I don't think they really care. They've given up on me. I don't care anyway. I've had enough of parents.'

He looked sad, Amina thought. Maybe he did care really. Maybe he was just pretending.

'Mama Luminita,' Leyla said suddenly, breaking the silence. 'Perhaps she can help Amina.'

4

'And where do you think you're running to?'

They stared at Leyla.

'Who?' Paul asked.

'Mama Luminita. She is a very wise woman,' Leyla said. 'A very strange wise woman. She cannot read or write but she remembers everything. She knows many things.'

'Do you think she knows where my mother is?' Amina asked.

'Perhaps. They say she can tell things about you just by looking at you. She knows things— you cannot understand how she knows these things.'

'Spooky,' Paul said.

'Maybe there is something she knows. I will find out if you can visit her. She lives a long

39

way from here and you must not tell anyone about her. Do you understand?'

Amina nodded.

'It is important,' Leyla said. 'You must not talk about her to anyone.'

'I promise,' Amina said.

'Can I come, too?' Paul said.

'I will ask,' Leyla said. 'I will let you know. Perhaps on Saturday night we can go.'

'That's your birthday, Amina,' Paul said.

'Be ready Saturday night,' Leyla said. 'Meanwhile write to your Aunt Victoria. She will be worried to the bottom of her boots.'

Paul and Amina laughed.

'I'll write today,' Amina said.

As they were leaving the café, Amina suddenly remembered. 'We haven't paid for the breakfasts,' she said.

Leyla laughed. 'Don't worry,' she said. 'Mrs Onen will take it off Paul's wages.'

'I'll pay for mine,' Amina insisted.

'No, I'm feeling generous today,' Paul said. 'Anyway, you're going to need all your money.'

When they got back to the house, Paul gave her a sheet of paper from his exercise book and she settled herself on the mattress and tried to compose a letter. Paul left her there, saying he was going out to do a bit of scavenging.

'Dear Auntie Vickie,' she wrote. 'I hope you are well. And Cleo and Lawrence. Don't worry about me. I'm fine. I'm going to find my mother. I'll come and see you but not yet. Thank you for looking after me. Love, Amina. PS I'm sorry about James. I didn't mean it. Honestly.'

Paul came back looking dirty and dishevelled and rather pleased with himself.

'Come and help me,' he said. 'I can't get it through the window.'

'What?'

'Come and see.'

It was an old mattress. Paul folded the two sides together and pushed it into the open window while Amina tugged it through from inside the house.

'Where'd you get it?' Amina asked.

'I found it on the skip in the next street. I found some other things, too. Look.'

He held up a filthy old sleeping bag, a battered kettle, two chipped plates, a coronation mug, and an electric toaster.

'It's amazing the things people throw away,' he said.

'The sleeping bag's disgusting,' Amina said.

'It just needs a bit of a clean,' he said. 'I've slept in worse. What do you think of the toaster?'

'Fantastic. Only it's not much use without electricity, is it?'

'You never know,' he said. 'We might have electricity one day.'

Amina gave Paul the letter for Leyla to post. She stayed in the house for the next few days to avoid being seen on the streets. Soon it would be the school holidays and it would be safer for her to go out. Paul brought back food and takeaways and made cheese sandwiches and cups of tea with water boiled in the kettle on the primus. He gave her books to read and tried to teach her a few chords on the guitar but she said it hurt her fingers too much. In the evenings, Paul went to work in the café and Amina sat on her mattress feeling lost and lonely. She made up songs and sang them to herself to pass the time. She dozed and dreamed of sunshine and fields of flowers and children who were her friends. Sometimes, she longed to be back at Auntie Vickie's where there was a proper bed and clean sheets and a bath with hot water and towels. Paul didn't seem to notice the dirt and discomfort but she felt as if she was drowning in dirt. Her skin itched and she had the impression that insects were crawling all over her. At night, she was still haunted by the dream of running and not moving, of hands reaching out to clutch her, of the sea sucking her under.

On Thursday night, Paul came back from the café, poked his head round the door of her room and sang out in a loud voice, 'We're off to see Mama What's-her-name.'

Amina struggled out of a troubled sleep and stared at him. 'What? What's the matter?'

'It's on,' Paul said. 'Leyla told me. We're meeting Mama What's-her-name. Saturday night. A van's picking us up. Aren't you pleased?'

'I'm asleep,' Amina groaned. She dived under the blankets and curled herself into a ball. Paul was a lot older than her but sometimes he acted like a little boy, even younger than she was.

It was a different dream. She was a prisoner in a room high up in a castle. It was dark and dirty and there were cobwebs everywhere. She was frightened of the rats and she couldn't escape. From the window she could see down below an army of men in black uniforms marching backwards and forwards. Then she heard whispers. 'Mama Luminita, Mama Luminita,' the whispers said. The whispers were in the room. The whispers were in her head. She struggled to drag herself out of the

43

dream but it was impossible. The guards stopped marching and looked up. Then she saw a dark shape flying through the air, flying towards her. Mama Luminita. The window opened and Mama Luminita held out her hand. She took it and the next moment they were flying together away from the castle, away from the men in black uniforms. She wasn't afraid. Mama Luminita was holding her hand. She tried to make out her face but she couldn't. It was always turned away from her. Silently she asked Mama Luminita, 'Please. I want to see your face.' The dark shape turned towards her, turned her face towards her but at that moment a flash of sunlight blinded her eyes and she saw nothing.

She woke with a start and saw that the sun had broken through at last and was sweeping away the layers of cloud. Amina jumped to her feet. She felt charged with new energy. She couldn't stay cooped up any longer. By midday, the last grey cobweb had been brushed away leaving a perfectly clean sky. She had to get out into the open, to feel the sun on her skin.

Paul was in what he called the music room, picking out a tune on his guitar.

'I dreamed about Mama Luminita last night,' Amina said.

Paul didn't look up from his guitar. 'What was she like?' he asked. 'Was she a witch?'

'I couldn't see her face,' Amina said. 'She rescued me. She made me fly.'

'On a broomstick?' Paul said.

'No. She just took my hand and I could fly.'

'Maybe she is a witch,' Paul said.

'I don't believe in witches,' Amina said. 'Anyway, I'm going for a walk. I'm going mad with boredom in this house.'

'Take care,' he said.

She climbed out through the back window and looked around her. What had once been a lawn was now a tangle of waist-high grass sprinkled with yellow dandelions in the middle of which was a black patch where someone had lit a bonfire. The small yard at the front of the house looked as if it had been used as a rubbish dump. It was overflowing with bulging black sacks, bottles, old newspapers, and empty cartons.

Once in the street, she began to run. She didn't know where she was running to. She just wanted to feel the wind on her face and in her hair. She wanted to stretch her limbs and release all her pent-up energy. She wanted to run till she left behind the grimy streets and rubbish-filled gardens and found herself in open fields and hills, run till she reached the sea and heard the gulls calling and the wind singing. She hardly noticed the women with their shopping bags who looked at her strangely as they dodged out of her way. She hardly noticed the blue car that was parked opposite the Crescent Moon café half a street in front of her. And as for the two men in identical dark blue suits who climbed out of the car and stood on the pavement ahead of her, she hardly noticed them. Until she almost collided with them.

'Well, little miss,' one of the men said, holding her arm in a tight grip. 'And where do you think you're running to?'

Amina looked up at his heavy red face, his thick lips, and the black hairs jutting out of his nose and felt her heart race. He was the horrible man who'd questioned her at the café. She was panting, trying to catch her breath. What was she to do?

'I think you'd better come with us,' the second man said, gripping her other arm.

She looked at them hopelessly, struggling to free herself.

'Don't try and pretend you don't understand English,' the red-faced man said. 'Who are you running from? You've been thieving, haven't you? Shoplifting.'

Amina shook her head.

'Then why are you running?'

'I . . . I like running,' Amina stammered.

The men laughed and propelled her towards the car. They pushed her inside onto the back seat. Redface climbed in beside her. The other man swung himself into the driving seat and drove off.

'What's this?' Redface said, pulling at the gold chain round her neck.

Amina pushed him away. 'Nothing,' she said. 'Leave me alone. I haven't done anything. Where are you taking me?'

'She speaks good English, doesn't she?' Redface said. 'For a foreigner. Why did you pretend you didn't know English?'

'I didn't,' Amina said.

'You didn't? You didn't? You naughty little liar. And you pretended to be that Kurdish girl's sister.'

'I didn't,' Amina said.

'Who are you then? Where do you come from?'

'I don't know,' Amina said.

'She doesn't know. Did you hear that, Jim? She doesn't know.'

'Go easy on her,' the driver said. 'She's only a child.'

Redface ignored him. 'Well, I'll tell you who you are, little miss. You're an illegal, aren't you? Outstayed your welcome. Not supposed to be here. Disobeyed orders. Should have been sent packing. Back to where you came from. With the rest of your family.' Then pushing his red face close to hers, he yelled, 'Where's the rest of your family? Mother? Father? Sisters? Brothers? Where are they hiding?'

Amina turned away to look out of the window. She had to stop this man shouting at her and asking her questions.

'There's a place that I call nowhere, it's far across the sea—' she sang in a loud voice.

'None of that!' Redface said. 'No singing allowed.'

If only she could get the car to stop, she thought to herself, she might be able to escape.

'I need the toilet,' she said.

'You'll have to wait,' Redface said.

'I can't. I need the toilet now.'

'You'll wait till we arrive.'

'I can't.'

'Yes, you can.'

'I'll do it in the car.'

48

'Filthy thing,' Redface said, moving away from her.

But they didn't stop till they'd turned left onto a main street and pulled up outside a newsagent's shop. They practically carried her up the stairs next to the shop and into an office with its window fronting the main street.

'Sit down!' Redface ordered. 'We've got a few questions for you so I hope you're not going to be difficult.'

'I need the toilet,' Amina reminded him.

Redface hesitated but the other man motioned for him to take Amina to the toilet at the end of a narrow corridor.

'Hurry up!' Redface ordered, pushing her inside.

She locked the door and looked for the window. It was coated with dirt and obviously hadn't been opened for years. Anyway, she was on the first floor so it would be impossible to escape that way. She went on the toilet, pulled the chain, and waited. And waited. She could hear Redface moving heavily outside. He was clearly becoming impatient. She waited, not moving, making no noise.

'Hurry up, I said,' Redface called. 'What are you doing in there?'

Still she didn't move or speak. Redface banged on the door and rattled the door handle.

'Come on! Come out!'

Amina froze, hardly daring to breathe. She heard Redface swear, then throw himself against the door. It creaked but the lock held. She heard his heavy step as he took a run at the door and threw his weight against it. Again the lock held. She heard him retreat a little as if to take a longer run at the door. As quietly as she could, she reached over to the key and opened the lock. Then she squeezed into a corner of the room as far away from the door as possible. She heard the man run along the corridor and hurl himself with all his force against the door. It burst open and she had a brief glimpse of Redface as he fell sprawling against the toilet seat. Then she was out of the door, along the corridor, down the stairs, and out into the street before he could recover.

She hesitated, looked left and right, then made for a side street a short sprint away. There she found a terraced house with a front garden hidden by a wall and a high hedge. She darted into the garden and collapsed in a corner behind a wheelie bin. Her heart was beating so fast it sounded like a machine-gun in her ears. She prayed that Redface and his friend wouldn't find her. She hated them more than she'd ever hated anyone in her life, even James.

5

'Dust on the wind'

It took her hours of walking and watching out for blue cars and men in dark blue suits before she found her way back to the house. There was no sign of Paul. Perhaps he was out looking for her. She made herself comfortable on the mattress and tried to read the book Paul had lent her but the words kept dancing about in front of her eyes. She couldn't concentrate. She felt hot, thirsty, and a little light-headed. She'd rest a little before she went out again and bought herself a cold drink and something to eat. She lay back and pretended she was floating in the sky on a feather bed of white clouds. She remembered nothing more until she was woken the next morning by the sound of Paul's guitar. She jumped up and ran into the next room.

'You slept late,' Paul said. 'What happened to you yesterday?'

'Is today Saturday?' Amina asked. 'Is it today we're going to see Mama Luminita?'

'Tonight,' Paul said. 'Where did you get to yesterday? I got worried. I thought you'd been kidnapped.'

'I just went for a walk,' Amina said uneasily.

'Come on,' Paul said. 'Tell me the truth. Did you get lost or something?'

Amina felt irritated. What did it have to do with him?

'You're not my father,' she said. 'I can go for a walk if I like, can't I?'

Paul looked at her, a hurt expression on his face. He put the guitar down, stood up, and walked out of the room, mumbling something to himself.

Amina felt awful. She hadn't meant to hurt his feelings. And she knew she needed his help. But why did he have to keep asking her, wanting to know everything? She went downstairs to the kitchen where Paul was boiling a kettle on the primus. He ignored her.

'Sorry,' she said.

He didn't look at her or respond.

'I got caught,' she said. 'Those two men who came into the café. They caught me.'

Now he looked at her and she told him the whole story, how she'd been caught, how she'd escaped, how she'd found her way back to the house.

Paul didn't, as she'd hoped, congratulate her on her cleverness in managing to get away. He just told her that the van would be picking them up at ten o'clock that night and suggested that she should stay in until then.

'You don't want to miss your appointment with Mama What's-her-name, do you?' he said.

The day passed painfully slowly for Amina. Paul shut himself in his room. He hardly said a word to her. At tea-time he went out and brought back a pile of sandwiches from the café.

'Present from Mrs Onen,' he said. 'And I bought you something.'

He threw her a box of crayons and a pad of white paper to draw on. 'Thanks,' she said, smiling at him. 'Does this mean you've stopped being mad at me?'

'No,' he said. 'But I'm getting there.'

'Jeepers creepers,' she said.

She tried out the coloured pencils. Carefully, she drew a beautiful multi-coloured bird. She loved birds. Sometimes she believed she was really a bird who'd been trapped in the body of a girl. One day, she'd escape and fly away. She drew another bird. Green and yellow body. Blue and orange wings. Were there birds like that? She filled page after page with drawings of differently coloured birds. Rainbow birds. Sunbirds. Paradise birds. She tried to decide which bird she would be. An eagle, perhaps, soaring and gliding over oceans and deserts and mountains? No. She was a brown bird. A small brown bird.

She was so absorbed in what she was doing that she gave a little scream of surprise when Paul came into the room to tell her that the van had arrived.

'What've you been drawing?' he asked.

'Nothing,' she said.

She ripped all the pages of bird drawings out of the pad and screwed them up.

'What did you do that for?' Paul asked.

'Nothing,' she said. 'Come on. Let's go.'

He sighed and followed her down the stairs and out of the window. Leyla was waiting for them, holding the back doors of the van open. Amina caught a glimpse of the swarthy face and bushy moustache of the driver.

'In the back. Quick!' Leyla said. 'There are many police about.'

They scrambled in. There were cushions for them to sit on. Leyla locked the doors and the van screeched away.

'Do you know where we're going?' Amina asked.

'No,' Paul replied. 'Leyla isn't saying.'

The van rattled and bumped along. There were no windows so they couldn't see where they were. It seemed to Amina that they'd driven for miles and miles. Were they still in London? She started to sing to herself but stopped when she saw Paul looking at her and smiling.

'What's the matter?' she said.

'Nothing. You've got a good voice.'

'Better than yours anyway.'

'Go on then. Sing something.'

Amina took a deep breath and closed her eyes. 'Bullies and men in blue uniforms, I hate them,' she sang. 'May they explode like rotten apples. May they shrivel up like burnt matchsticks. May the hair in their noses choke them.'

'Wow!' exclaimed Paul. 'Fierce. We could go busking, you and me. You could sing and I'll play the guitar. Make some money. What do you think?'

Amina shook her head.

'Why not?'

'I don't sing for money,' she said. 'I sing for magic.'

The van stopped suddenly, jerking them off their seats. The back door was opened and they jumped out. They seemed to be in the countryside. There were no lights anywhere. There was no moon and the sky was brightly patterned with stars.

'There's the Great Bear,' Paul said pointing northwards.

'Where are we?' Amina asked.

'No questions,' Leyla said. 'Come. We walk from here.'

The van drove off. They followed a footpath through a field, skirted a clump of bushes, crawled under a barbed-wire fence and found themselves in what seemed like an apple orchard. On the other side of the orchard, Amina could make out a dark ruin of a building.

'Is that where we're going?' she asked. 'But it's dark. There's nobody there.'

'Come. Follow me,' Leyla said.

As they drew near to the building, Amina could see that, though the stone walls were still standing, a fire had burnt out half the roof and the windows were empty of glass.

Suddenly, a large shape jumped up in the entrance where there had once been a door and uttered a menacing growl. Amina started back with a little scream.

Leyla took her hand. 'He will not hurt you,' she said. 'And he knows me. Look.'

She held her hand out to the dog and crooned in a low musical voice, 'Hello, Brutus. Good dog, Brutus.'

The dog came towards her, sniffed her hand, and started to wag its tail.

'Come,' she said. 'We go into the house.'

'I don't understand,' Amina said as they stood in the abandoned farmhouse. 'There's nobody here. And it smells horrible.'

Paul walked about as if in a dream. 'It's amazing,' he said, staring through the open roof to the night sky. 'Amazing.'

Among the flagstones was a square wooden cover with a metal ring attached to it. Leyla pulled it open. 'There,' she said.

Amina peered down. There seemed to be a room down there. Candles were flickering. A rope ladder was hanging next to the opening. 'You go first, Amina,' Leyla said.

'What's there?' Amina asked, staring down into the candlelit gloom.

'You will see,' Leyla said. 'Go.'

Amina grabbed the rope, swung herself through the opening and, clinging on tight, made her way carefully down the ladder and onto the floor. She looked around her in amazement. She was in an enormous cellar lit by scores of candles. All around, hanging from the ceiling and the walls, were colourful carpets and curtains, some of them obviously serving to screen off parts of the cellar so as to form separate rooms. A circle of children, their faces swivelled round to stare at her, were sitting on a carpet. In the centre of the circle, seated on a wicker chair like a queen on her throne, was a stocky woman. She wore a long red skirt and around her shoulders a flowery shawl. Her face, though lined, was, thought Amina, still beautiful. Her eyes were dark. Fiery red lipstick marked out her mouth. Her long hair was black with heavy streaks of grey. Two large gold rings hung from her ears. Amina was conscious of eyes boring into her, examining her, but no one moved or spoke.

By this time, Paul and Leyla had joined her. Leyla went up to Mama Luminita and kissed her hand.

'This is Amina,' she said. 'The girl who is looking for her mother. And this is Paul. Her friend. He is English but he is a kind person and can be trusted.'

'Welcome,' Mama Luminita said in a husky voice. 'Sit.'

The three of them joined the circle of children. Amina looked around, examining the children's faces. Some were black, some brown, some white. There were some quite small children and others almost grown-up. Who were all these children? Had they all, like her, lost their mothers? And what was this strange place with its carpets and candles? She felt as if she was in somebody's dream.

A voice began to sing, a song with no words, a song that seemed to Amina so sad, so lost and lonely, that she felt her heart ache. Soon all the children were joining in, letting their voices flow into a river of sound that flooded the cellar. Then out of the sound of singing came Mama Luminita's voice.

'I am Mama Luminita,' she chanted. 'I am the dust that is blown on the wind, the dust blown this way and that way by the wind, blown across mountains and deserts and oceans. I have no home. No place on earth is my home. I wander the world, hoping for a word of welcome, looking for shelter from the wind. My people are poor people. We have nothing. We are the dust of the earth. But we are proud people. They come and they mock us and threaten us and attack us because we are proud, because we are different. Because we do not belong. They drive us out and so we are scattered like dust in a terrible wind to all corners of the earth. We settle here and there hoping for a word of welcome, looking for shelter and everywhere the wind comes and scatters us. We are dust blown on the wind, we are dust on the wind . . . '

And all the children took up the cry. 'We are dust, we are dust on the wind.'

Then the wordless song continued above which arose a child's voice, a young girl's voice. 'When the soldiers came we ran. We ran so fast we forgot to untie the dog. The dog was howling. While I was running I heard the howling of the dog. I wanted to run back and free the dog but my father said no. So the dog was howling. Then I heard a bang and the howling stopped. Sometimes I dream and in my dream I hear a dog howling and then, when I wake up, I cry because I know I am not at home and the dog is dead.'

Another voice cut through the singing, a boy's voice, Amina thought, although she couldn't see which child was speaking.

'When I first come to this country,' the voice said, 'people stare at me. They think I come from the moon or somewhere. They think I'm a moonboy. At school, the other children talk about me, they say bad things about me. They laugh at me because I don't speak English. The teachers help me learn English. Now I know English and I have friends. I'm not a moonboy any more. So when they tell my mother we must leave, go back to my old country, all the school say no. Ali must stay. He is our friend. Hands off our friend. I don't know what the ending will be.'

'I am Fatma,' a girl's voice sang out. 'I am from Turkey but I am not Turkish. My father said he was Kurdish so the police came and took him away. He was singing a song in Kurdish so they beat him.'

'I am Juan. From Colombia. This is what happened to me. Look.'

He held up his right hand and, peering into the candle-gloom, Amina saw with a shiver that the index finger and middle finger were missing.

'They did that to me. Chopped off my fingers. I am lucky. They killed my father. They killed my mother. They burned our house. They are called death squads. And so death came to the village. They said we were helping the rebels, the guerrillas, so they brought death to the village.'

A girl's voice. 'I am Radhika. From Sri Lanka. There is a war in my country. The rebel soldiers came and wanted to take my brother to be a soldier but my mother hid him. My brother was twelve. Then the government soldiers threatened us because they said we were helping the rebels. So we fled. We travelled to many countries. We spent all our money. In Moscow it was all snow. In Nigeria it was all hot. Now we want to stay in this country but the letter says no. The letter says we must go back where we came from. Appeal refused. I will not go back. I am frightened of the soldiers.'

'I am Ahmed from Somalia. Fighting and killing. That's all I remember. My friend's family was shot. His whole family. I don't know why. They were our neighbours. I used to cry. But people don't like you if you cry. So now I only cry in my head. I cannot say the things that are in my head. Fighting and killing. That's all I remember.'

'All my life has been war,' said another voice. 'I love my country, Afghanistan. My home. There was a garden. Melons grew. Now it is destroyed. What can I tell you? That they came, the fighters, to my school and killed children? You will not believe me. They did not believe me.'

'My name is Kadir. In Iraq they put me in prison. They beat me. They ask about my father, my mother, where are they. They do things to me. I don't want to think about it. When I come here, they ask me questions. How old are you? When I tell them, they do not believe me. They lock me up. They put me in another prison. They say it is not a prison. There are fences and barbed wire but they say it is not a prison. To me it is a prison. My head is full of ghosts. I don't want to think about it.'

The singing stopped. There was a silence like a long, sad sigh. Amina hoped there wouldn't be any more stories. She thought if she heard any more stories, she'd burst into tears. But again the wordless singing began and still the voices came.

'We had to leave Nigeria. I don't remember why. I know we were hungry. We walked and walked. I don't know how far. There were many of us walking. We had no food. We found leaves to eat. We drank from muddy pools. Some died. Many died. Sometimes we were in a truck. Sometimes we walked. I don't know how far. Crossing the desert was bad. Some died of thirst. I had fever. I don't remember. My uncle carried me, I think. We came to a great fence made of sharp wire. My uncle said this is still Africa but across the wire is Spain. Across the wire we are safe. The wire was sharp to cut you in two. I don't know how we crossed the wire. I don't know how I came here. I don't remember.'

'I am from Kosova. I came here without my heart. My heart is in my home. War came and bombs fell and the soldiers said we must leave. They blew up my house. My home. Now they say the war is over, go back home. What home? Home is gone. Friends dead. There is nothing. I have lost my heart.'

'Where I come from, they call us gypsies. They call us black swine. Gangs attacked us. They had knives and chains and baseball bats. The police laughed. They did nothing. Gangs came and threw petrol bombs at our house. My brother, Josef, was burnt to death. So we left. We travelled through many countries. We paid a man to take us in a motor boat to Italy. It was night. I was frightened. I thought we would drown. When we came here, they asked us questions and questions and questions. Then they put us in a damp room. All of us. We were frightened to go out. Gangs attacked us. They had knives and chains. They called us scum. They called us gypsies. When the letter came, it said we had to go back. Go back home. We have no home. So I ran away. Luba's my name. From the Roma people.'

'War, sickness, food,' said another voice. 'We came in a lorry. Police were everywhere. It was my brother's fault. They saw his arm sticking out. They say, Why do you come here? I say I am hungry. I want to study. They say no. Go back home. Go back to Africa. You are illegal. You cannot stay here. I say, Why? You have plenty food. You eat too much. We have nothing. That is not fair. Here food is everywhere. Too much. Where is our food? It must be you have taken our share. You have stolen our food. Then I ran away.'

And then, above the sound of the singing children's voices, another voice arose, an eerie, mournful voice which startled Amina and sent a chill of fear through her body. It was and it wasn't the voice of a child. Where was it coming from? She looked at Paul. His face was tense and more pale than she'd ever seen it. Leyla was staring at the floor. She had tears in her eyes.

'Weep for me,' the voice said. 'Weep for me for I am nothing. My name is nobody. They killed me. They killed me twice.'

And then Amina saw that Mama Luminita was staring wildly upwards in a kind of trance and the scarlet gash of her mouth was open and from it bubbled this strange, mournful voice.

'They killed me,' it said. 'First they killed me with hunger. Then they killed me with bullets. They killed me twice. My name is nobody. I am a life that will never be lived. I am all children whose lives will never be lived. Weep for us. Weep for us.'

Amina folded her arms over her face and sobbed.

6

'You were screaming. Why were you screaming?'

She wept until she could weep no more and the flow of tears dried up. She felt the warmth of Leyla's body against hers and the comfort of Leyla's arms around her. She was sure everyone was staring at her. She felt stupid crying like that. Why was she crying? What did she have to cry about?

'It's all right, Amina, it's all right,' Leyla whispered. 'Tell Mama Luminita your story. Tell her.'

Amina raised her head and opened her eyes. All the children were watching Mama Luminita who was holding out her hands to her and smiling.

'Come, Amina,' she said. 'Here we are your

friends. All of us here. Yes?'

There was a murmur of assent.

'You are our sister, our daughter, our family. Talk to us. Tell us. We are listening.'

Amina took a deep breath. 'I am Amina,' she said. 'I don't know where I come from. I don't remember.'

Slowly, hesitantly at first, then more confidently, Amina unfolded her story. There was an intense listening silence while she talked. Finally, she said, 'It was seven years ago today. That's when I came to this country. That's what Aunt Victoria told me. Now I want to find my mum. I miss her.'

There was a moment's silence followed by a buzz of noise. Mama Luminita was staring upwards as if looking for inspiration.

'Seven years ago,' Mama Luminita began. 'A night of blackness. The sea rough. A motor boat rocking through the waves. Packed with refugees. Men. Women. Children. Frightened that the boat will sink. A woman is clutching her child, her small daughter, to her. She is praying. The boat drives towards the beach. The engine stops. The boatman orders the passengers out. Out into the sea. They are struggling now, struggling against the waves, treading water, wading towards the shore. The small children are lifted up over the waves. They are whimpering but they have been told to make no noise. One woman slips, disappears, swept away by the waves. The boat turns, makes off into the night.

'The refugees reach the shore, cold, wet, shivering. The police are waiting for them. They are taken to be questioned, to be given hot drinks and questioned. They do not understand the questions. They come from Iran, Iraq, Turkey. Their fingerprints are taken. Their photographs are taken. They are locked up until people are found who can translate for them. They tell their stories. War, hunger, torture, lives destroyed. They ask for refuge. They are put in a hostel. It is not a nice place. The newspapers call them names. Bogus. They are frightened to go out. People give them bad looks. Sometimes the men are attacked.

'Time passes. A few are allowed to stay. The rest must be deported. Are they sent back? I can't say. Some go but others are too frightened. One man says he would rather die than go back to his country. They do not believe him. One night he hangs himself. Then they believe. Some run away. Disappear—

who knows where? Who knows? Dust blown on the wind.'

'How do you know all this?' Amina asked. 'I mean about the boat and everything.'

Mama Luminita tapped her forehead. 'In here,' she said. 'I hold the history of those who suffer in here. I remember everything.' Then she put her hand on her heart. 'And their pain,' she said, 'their pain I hold in here.'

'The woman who was swept away,' Amina said in a tiny voice. 'Was that my mother?'

Mama Luminita shook her head. 'She was not holding a child,' she said. 'But this is strange. I have not heard anywhere of a mother searching for her lost child, for her lost daughter, for a daughter called Amina. I have not heard that. So, Amina, I think your Aunt Victoria knows something. I think she knows more than she has told you. You must ask her. You must go and ask her to tell you the truth. Only the truth.'

'I don't know,' Amina said. 'I don't know.'

'It is the only way. She knows. I am sure of it.'

The trapdoor was pulled open and all eyes turned to see the dark face of a man with a thick moustache peering down at them.

'Leyla,' he called.

Leyla stood up. 'We must go,' she said. 'The van is waiting.'

She took Amina's hand. 'Say thank you to Mama Luminita,' she said.

Amina stood there awkwardly, unable to speak. Her mouth was dry. The rose-scented smell of Mama Luminita's perfume made her feel slightly sick. She opened her mouth but no words would come.

Mama Luminita reached out a hand and stroked Amina's cheek. 'You will find your mother,' she said. 'I know it. Be strong.'

'Stay with us, Amina,' a child's voice called. And the cry was taken up by the other children. 'Stay with us, Amina. Stay with us.'

Amina shook her head. 'Thank you,' she said. 'Thank you. I have to find my mother.'

She ran to the rope ladder and climbed up. At the top, she looked back to see Paul and Leyla following her and the upturned faces of the children looking at her solemnly.

She waved to them. 'Goodbye,' she called.

'Goodbye,' they chorused back. 'Come back soon.'

No one spoke as they made their way back to the van. Amina's head was buzzing with questions that she didn't know how to ask.

It wasn't until they were bumping along in

the van on the journey home that Paul broke the silence. 'That's the weirdest thing I've ever seen,' he said. 'If I write it in my book, nobody'll believe me.'

'It was sad,' Amina said. 'All those stories. Dust blown on the wind. But I don't understand. Who looks after the children? Where are their mums and dads?'

Paul shrugged. 'It seems like Mama Luminita's become their mum now. Anyway, I expect they're pretty good at looking after themselves.'

'She was strange, wasn't she?' Amina said. 'When she was calling out, "Weep for us, weep for us," it made me go all shivery. But she didn't help me, did she? She didn't tell me where my mum is.'

'She told you how you came to England,' Paul said. 'And she told you to ask your Aunt Victoria to tell you the truth.'

'How can I?' Amina said. 'I don't want to be put in prison.'

Paul laughed. 'Don't be daft. Why should they put you in prison? For stabbing James in the arm? Jeepers creepers, they don't put you in prison for things like that.'

'For being illegal then.'

'Course not,' Paul said. 'Anyway you don't

have to go back to see her. You can ask her to meet you in London. At the café. That would be a good place. I'll arrange it if you like.'

'I dunno,' Amina said. 'I'm too tired to think.'

'Otherwise, what are you going to do? How will you ever find your mum? You've got to talk to Auntie Vic.'

The van pulled up sharply. Leyla opened the back doors to let them out.

'Home at last,' Paul said.

'It's not my home,' Amina said.

'It's all you've got,' Paul said.

'Quick,' Leyla said. 'There's nobody about.'

She gave Amina a hug and waved them into the house.

'In my home,' Amina said as she was climbing through the window, 'I'll be able to go in through the front door.'

Paul was already halfway through the window when he heard loud voices in the street breaking the silence of the night. He hesitated, then dropped back into the garden and ran round to the front of the house. He saw two youths standing next to the van, yelling abuse. Leyla was trying to open the passenger door of the van. Every time she opened it, the youths pushed it shut again. One of them carried a can of beer which he was waving in Leyla's face. She was screaming at them to go away. The driver climbed out of the van and walked towards the two youths. He was a big burly man and he carried what looked to Paul like a large spanner. The two youths backed away. The driver waited for Leyla to climb into the van. Then he jumped into the driving seat. The van skidded away. One of the youths swore loudly and threw the beer can after it.

Paul raced back into the house and ran up the stairs. Amina was at the window.

'What's happening?' she said. 'Who are they?'

'I don't know,' Paul said. 'They're drunk.'

Now the youths were pointing at the house. They seemed to be arguing with each other.

'I don't like them,' Amina said. 'Suppose they try and get into the house.'

'I hope not,' Paul said.

'Can't you lock the window?'

Paul shook his head.

One of the youths picked up a stone and threw it at the house. It clattered against one of the boarded-up downstairs windows.

'Rule Britannia,' the other one sang in an out-of-tune voice.

'It's all right,' Paul said. 'They're going.'

They watched the two youths weave their way down the street, trailing their drunken voices behind them.

Amina took off her trainers and crawled under the blankets.

'I hope they don't come back,' she said.

'Shouldn't think so,' Paul said. 'Goodnight.'

It was still dark when Amina woke, writhing and sweating. Paul was shaking her, calling her name.

'What? Whassamatter?' she said. 'Go away.'

'You were screaming,' Paul said. 'Were you having a nightmare?'

Amina sat up, wrapping a blanket tightly round her shoulders. 'My mother,' she said. 'She was there. I saw her.'

'What did she look like?' Paul asked.

'I don't know now. You woke me up. She's gone now.'

'You were screaming,' Paul said. 'Why were you screaming?'

'Auntie Victoria was there, too. Somebody like Auntie Victoria. I don't know where we were. Auntie Victoria and my mother. They were fighting. They were hitting each other. The woman who looked like Auntie Victoria was hitting my mother. I thought she was going to kill her. I was shouting, "Stop it! Stop it!" It was horrible.'

'Just a dream,' Paul said gently.

Amina shivered. 'Is it morning soon?' she asked.

'No. I'd only just gone to sleep when I heard you screaming.'

'What am I going to do?' Amina said.

'Talk to Auntie Victoria,' Paul said. 'I told you. I'll arrange it.'

'I don't know. I'm frightened.'

'You won't go to prison,' Paul said.

'Not that. I'm not frightened of that.'

'What then?'

'What she might tell me. I'm frightened of what she might tell me.'

'I don't understand. Don't you want to find your mother?'

'Maybe I don't. Maybe it's a bad idea.'

'But—'

They were silent for a time, deep in their own thoughts.

'Well,' Paul sighed. 'I think we should go to sleep. You'll feel better in the morning.'

'I don't want to dream any more,' Amina said.

'Maybe when you've found your mother, you won't have any more of these dreams.'

'Do you think so?'

'Maybe.'

'Jeepers creepers,' Amina said, settling back on the mattress and pulling the blanket over her head.

'Goodnight,' Paul said.

The next time Amina woke up, it was day and Paul was shaking her again.

'What now?' she said. 'Stop shaking me.'

'Pack your bag,' Paul said. 'We've got to leave.'

'What? Why?'

'Just do it,' Paul ordered and went into the room next door.

Something urgent in his voice made her jump. She hurriedly put on her trainers and pushed her few belongings into her bag. Paul came back carrying his guitar and shoulder bag.

'Why are we running away?' Amina asked.

'Can't you hear them? Come over to the window. But don't let them see you.'

Amina crawled along the floor and peeped through the dirt-stained window. A crowd of people were outside the house, shouting and carrying placards. Most of them were young men. The only placard she could read said, 'Scum. Send them back.'

'Is it them?' she asked. 'From last night?'

'I suppose so,' Paul said. 'Them and their friends. They think we're refugees. They probably think the house is full of refugees.'

A policeman and a policewoman appeared and started to talk to the men who were pointing towards the house.

'Time to go,' Paul said.

He slung the bag over his shoulder and they ran downstairs. Just as they were about to climb out through the window, Amina saw Paul run back into the kitchen and return carrying the toaster.

'What do you want that for?'

'You never know,' Paul said.

'You're mad,' Amina said.

Amina climbed out first and took the toaster and the guitar while Paul followed her into the garden. They waded through the long grass, stepped over the broken fence at the end of the garden and found themselves on a narrow path. Paul led the way left along the path till they reached the street.

'Pity,' he said. 'I was getting quite fond of that house.'

'I wasn't,' Amina said. 'Where are we going?'

'To the Crescent Moon,' Paul said. 'We can have breakfast there. And leave our stuff till we find somewhere else to stay.'

'What if those horrible men raid it again?'

'Shouldn't think so,' Paul said. 'Not on a Sunday.'

The café wasn't very busy when they arrived. At one table, Amina observed, were the men who'd run off when the café had been raided the last time she'd been there. One of them, she thought, was the driver of the van which had taken them to see Mama Luminita. Mrs Onen was there, of course, large and expressionless, sitting behind the cash register. And Leyla, looking hot and tired, was carrying plates of breakfast. She barely glanced at them as they settled at a table by the window but when she'd finished serving, she came over to them with a quizzical look on her face.

'What's this?' she said pointing at the guitar and the toaster.

Paul told her what had happened.

'What now?' she asked. 'Where will you stay?'

Paul shrugged. 'There are always empty houses,' he said. 'Can we have some breakfast?'

When Leyla came back with Paul's bacon sandwich and Amina's baked beans on toast, she told them she'd spoken to Mrs Onen. 'She can't give you anywhere to stay,' she said, 'but you can leave your things here if you like. Till you find somewhere.'

'Is Mrs Onen Kurdish, too?' Amina asked.

'No. She's Turkish,' Leyla replied.

'I thought Kurdish people didn't like Turkish people.'

'People are people,' Leyla said. 'Mrs Onen, too, is a refugee. Many years ago she came here. In Turkey she was in prison. For trying to organize workers. At that time she was very active in politics. But the government didn't like her politics.'

Amina looked across at the heavy figure of Mrs Onen who hadn't moved from her chair behind the cash register since they'd been in the café. She couldn't imagine Mrs Onen being active in anything.

'What's politics?' she asked.

'Politics? Politics is everything,' Leyla said. 'You are politics. I am politics. Politics is what the Turkish police did to me. Politics is filling in forms and answering questions I don't understand so I can stay in this country, so I can have some peace from politics.'

'I don't understand,' Amina said.

'I also don't understand,' Leyla said.

After breakfast, Leyla led them behind the counter and upstairs to a small room which was full of cardboard boxes.

'Your things will be safe here,' she said. 'But as you see—' Suddenly she stopped and her body stiffened. 'What is happening?'

From downstairs came the sound of men's voices shouting angrily. There was a crash like the sound of glass shattering.

'Wait here,' she ordered.

She ran down the stairs and a minute later ran back up, crying, 'Trouble. Always trouble in this country. This, too, is politics.'

'It's those men, isn't it?' Paul said. 'The ones who were outside our house.'

'They want to kill us,' Leyla said. 'Someone has thrown a brick through the window. Mrs Onen is phoning the police. There will be fighting. Stupid. They are stupid with their stupid insults. What harm have we done them?'

'What shall we do?' Amina said.

'Take your bags. Go out through the kitchen into the yard. There is a door there that leads to the street at the back.'

'My guitar—' Paul began.

'It will be safe here,' Leyla said. 'I promise.'

At the bottom of the stairs, Amina heard furious shouts and curses and the sound of furniture being thrown about. She glimpsed the bulky figure of Mrs Onen standing by the counter holding a frying pan in one hand and defying anyone to pass. They ran into the kitchen past two frightened-looking men in white overalls and dashed into the yard. Then they were through the door and out into a narrow alleyway.

Amina felt herself trembling. 'Running,' she said. 'Always running.'

'Yes,' said Paul with a smile. 'Like dust blown on the wind.'

7

'She didn't love me. Why didn't she love me?'

They took the tube to Hampstead and walked up the hill to the Heath. Amina was delighted by the trees, the grass, the open space.

'It's like the countryside,' she said. 'Not like London at all.'

'When I first came to London,' Paul said, 'I used to sleep out on the Heath. Made myself a bed of grass and ferns. Then it got too cold and damp. And I started hearing things.'

'What sort of things?'

'Ghostly noises,' Paul said. 'I saw a spaceship once.'

'You didn't.'

'Yes, I did. It landed in that field over there. And do you know who climbed out of it?'

'Who?'

'Refugees from outer space asking for asylum.'

'Ha ha. Very funny.'

'True,' Paul said. 'You'll read it in my book when I'm a famous writer.'

They walked on until they came to a big white house overlooking a field where families were enjoying the sunshine and children were playing football and throwing frisbees. The field sloped down to a lake and Amina walked to the lake's edge and stared at the water.

'Don't fall in,' Paul said.

She turned round and Paul saw the scowl on her face.

'What's the matter?' he said.

'You said you were going to help me find my mother,' she shouted at him accusingly.

'All right,' he said, taken aback. 'I'm going to phone your Aunt Victoria, aren't I?'

'What are you going to phone her for?'

'I'll say you want to meet her, to talk to her.'

Amina squatted by the lake and threw sticks and stones into the water, rippling the reflected sunlight. Two ducks circled round hoping for bread.

'I wish I was a duck,' Amina said. 'I wish I didn't have to think about what to do.'

Paul knelt beside her and said gently, 'Look, Amina. Give me Aunt Vic's phone number. If she's in, I'll ask her to come to London today and meet us—I mean meet you here.'

'She won't come.'

'Yes, she will. What's her number?'

'She won't want to talk to me anyway. Not after what I've done.'

'What's her number, Amina?' Paul said between gritted teeth.

Amina told him and he wrote it down in his exercise book.

'Wait here,' he said. 'I have to find a phone box. I won't be long.'

Amina watched the ducks bobbing down under the water, their tails sticking up in the air. A small boy, barely able to walk, wobbled his way to the lake, holding tightly on to his mother's hand. His mother gave him some bread which he dropped into the water. The ducks darted forward, beaks open, and grabbed the bread. The boy laughed. His mother gave him another piece of bread. He held it out to Amina.

'Here,' he said.

She took the bread and lobbed it into the lake. Again the little boy laughed as the ducks gobbled the bread. He gave Amina another piece of bread which she threw at the ducks, then another and another until all the bread was gone.

'All gone, Benjamin,' his mother said.

'All gone,' Benjamin said.

'Benjamin thinks you look sad,' his mother said to Amina. 'Are you all by yourself?'

'I'm waiting for my friend,' Amina said.

'You shouldn't look so worried at your age,' the woman said. 'Look at the sunlight on the water. Isn't it beautiful?'

Amina shrugged.

'What's your name?'

Amina didn't want to answer but it seemed rude not to. 'Amina,' she said.

'That's a nice name, isn't it, Benjamin?' his mother said. 'Say goodbye to Amina, Benjamin.'

''Bye,' Benjamin said, holding out a chubby hand.

Amina held it for a moment. ''Bye,' she said.

She watched as they walked away, the mother pushing the buggy with one hand and holding Benjamin's hand with the other. She went back to the field, lay down on the grass, and stared at the blue sky and the fluffy white clouds sailing across. She closed her eyes and was just dozing off when she heard Paul's voice.

'There you are,' he said.

She opened her eyes and saw him standing over her. He was out of breath.

'I didn't see you at first,' he said. 'I thought you'd gone.'

Amina sat up. 'Did you speak to her? Auntie Victoria?'

'She's coming,' Paul said. 'She's coming. She was crying when I told her. Really crying. She said she'd catch the first train to London. She kept thanking me. She'll meet us at three o'clock by the white house. I said she'd come, didn't I? She seemed really excited.'

'I thought you said she was crying.'

'Excited and crying. She asked if you were coming home.'

'What did you tell her?'

'I said I didn't know. I said you wanted to talk to her first. About your mother and everything.'

'What did she say?'

'I told you. She's meeting us at three o'clock.'

'What's the time now?'

Paul opened his shoulder bag and took out his clock. 'Lucky I remembered this,' he said. 'It's quarter to twelve.'

'Three hours to wait,' Amina said.

'I'll get burnt if I stay in the sun,' Paul said. 'There's a café over there. Let's go and have a drink and a sandwich.'

Amina stood up and grinned at him. 'Thanks for phoning Auntie Vickie,' she said. 'I couldn't have done it.'

They took their sandwiches outside to eat under a tree. Afterwards, they went for a walk in the wood. Then they sat under the tree again and played I Spy. They played guessing games. They played guessing what the other was thinking. Every so often they played guessing the time. Whoever was nearest won 1p.

'Still another hour,' Amina said.

'I wish I had my guitar,' Paul said. 'My fingers feel nervous.'

'I feel nervous all over,' Amina said.

'Sing me a song,' Paul said.

'What for?'

'Sing me a lullaby,' Paul said lying back on the grass. 'I feel sleepy.'

Amina lay back, too, and began to sing in a low voice: 'There's a place that I call nowhere. It's far across the sea—'

'Sing on,' Paul said.

'There's a woman there who's singing . . . '

Amina looked across at Paul. His eyes were closed. He was breathing heavily. He seemed to be fast asleep. His face, tilted towards her, looked so white and drawn, she thought he looked ill. His fair hair was longer now, and uncombed. He needed a bath.

'Hello,' said a voice. 'You found your friend then.'

Amina looked up at Benjamin's mother. Benjamin, she noticed, was sitting in his buggy, cramming a half-eaten ice cream into his mouth.

'Yes,' Amina said. 'Actually, he's my brother.'

The woman laughed. 'Really? He doesn't look like your brother.'

'You can't always tell by looks,' Amina said, closing her eyes in an attempt to avoid further questions.

'True,' Benjamin's mother said. 'Well, sweet dreams.'

Amina woke with a start, her head thick with a half-remembered dream, and looked across at Paul who was just opening his eyes.

'What's the time?' she asked.

He sat up and took the clock out of his bag. 'Ten past three.'

She looked towards the benches alongside

90

the white house. People were sitting there but it was difficult to see if Aunt Victoria was one of them. She grabbed her bag and ran up the slope. Paul followed behind.

At the top of the slope, she heard a little scream and saw a stout woman running to meet her, arms outstretched, her handbag swinging wildly. The next moment she was being squeezed against Aunt Victoria's ample body.

'Amina, Amina, my baby,' Aunt Victoria cried. 'You bad girl.'

Amina stiffened. She felt a tear trickle onto her forehead. She breathed the familiar scent of Aunt Victoria's perfume and nearly choked. 'You're suffocating me,' she said.

'Let me look at you.' She released Amina from her embrace and examined her. 'Your hair,' she said. 'What have you done to it? You look as if you've been sleeping in a dustbin.'

'This is Paul,' Amina said as she saw him approaching them. 'He's my friend. He's the one who phoned you.'

'Hello, Paul,' Aunt Victoria said and, holding on to Amina's arm, she led her to an empty bench and sat her down.

Paul stood there looking lost, then sat himself

under a magnolia tree on the grassy slope, took a book from his bag and began to read.

'What's all this about?' Aunt Victoria demanded. 'Where have you been? Why did you run away? Don't you know how worried I was?'

'I went to find my mother,' Amina said sullenly. 'You're not my mother.'

'I see,' Aunt Victoria said, looking hurt. 'And did you find your mother?'

'Mama Luminita said—'

'Who?'

'Mama Luminita knows about refugees. She remembers everything. She said you knew the truth. She said you hadn't told me the truth. I want to know. I want to know who I am. Everything.'

'I see,' Aunt Victoria said again.

There was a silence while Amina waited for Aunt Victoria to say something, to explain, but Aunt Victoria seemed dumbstruck. She was examining Amina's face as if trying to see into her thoughts.

'I'm not coming back,' Amina said. 'Not if you don't tell me.'

Aunt Victoria sighed deeply. She took Amina's hand and held it in both of hers. 'You mustn't blame me,' she said. 'It's not my fault.'

'What isn't?'

'Listen,' Aunt Victoria began. 'When I found you on my doorstep, it was something so strange and magical—almost as if God had sent you to me—such a beautiful little girl. Then, when I heard about the refugees, I realized that you must have belonged to one of them. So I tried to find your mother. I told you that.'

'Yes,' said Amina.

'And I told you that I didn't find her—your mother.'

'Yes,' said Amina.

'Well, that wasn't quite true.'

Amina snatched her hand away and folded her arms. Her face was set hard. 'You lied to me. Why did you lie to me?'

'Wait a minute, Amina, it's not as simple as that.'

'What then?'

'When I found your mother, they'd put her in an awful hostel. There were three women and a baby in one room. She was the only one who spoke some English, quite good English. She was lost, frightened, and alone. She had no money, just vouchers which hardly gave her enough to live on. She showed me the form she was supposed to fill in to apply for political asylum. You understand what that means?'

'I think so.'

'She was in despair. I tried to help her fill it in. But I think she'd given up. She was sure they wouldn't let her stay. They were going to send her back.'

'Back? Back where?'

'Patience, Amina. All in good time. So she said— How can I explain this? She asked me—she begged me to take care of you. To give you a good life. "I don't know what's going to happen to me." I still remember her words. "Look after my little girl. She will have a better life with you." That's what she said.'

Amina's mouth turned down and she began to cry. 'She didn't love me. Why didn't she love me?'

'She loved you, Amina, of course she did,' Aunt Victoria said, putting her arm around the girl. 'She still loves you.'

'Why did she give me away then?'

'It's not black and white like that, Amina. People make decisions, difficult decisions— Do you think it was easy? People do things—they do what they think is best. You mustn't blame her.'

Amina nestled her head on Aunt Victoria's shoulder.

'It's no one's fault, Amina,' Aunt Victoria said.

'It is. It's someone's fault. It's not fair. Things like that shouldn't happen.'

'No, they shouldn't,' sighed Aunt Victoria. 'But they do. And she didn't give you away. She said, "Look after my little girl. But not forever. Not forever." That's what she said.'

'Did she?'

'Yes. That's why I never adopted you. I gave her my telephone number and address for when she wanted you back. Until then, I promised I'd take care of you.'

Amina disentangled herself from Aunt Victoria and dried her eyes. 'Why didn't you tell me this before?' she demanded.

'What good would it have done? It would have just upset you.'

'I still don't understand,' Amina said. 'Where did my mum come from? Where do I belong?'

'I can't tell you that, Amina, because I don't really know. And that's the truth. I think the other refugees in the group came from Iraq or Turkey. Somewhere like that. But your mother never said. She was very vague when I asked her. I don't know why.'

'So I don't belong anywhere,' Amina said.

'Don't you feel you belong here? With me? I've tried to make you feel at home.'

Amina shook her head. 'I need to know,' she said. 'I need to know where I came from in the beginning.'

'Well,' Aunt Victoria smiled, 'you'll be able to ask your mother that now.'

Amina jumped, startled. She couldn't believe what she'd heard. 'What? But . . . but where is she?'

'You haven't let me tell you the rest of the story yet,' Aunt Victoria said. 'I went to visit your mother twice in the hostel. The third time I went she'd gone. Disappeared. No one knew where she'd gone or if they did, they weren't saying. I couldn't find out anything— whether she'd been deported, whether she'd just run away somewhere. And that's how it was for years. Silence. But I thought of her a lot. I kept expecting her to come back. Whenever there was a ring at the door, I thought it was your mother come to take you away. Because I didn't want to lose you. I love you like my own, Amina, you know that.'

'But she didn't come back. She never did. Did she?'

'One week ago,' Aunt Victoria said, 'just after you ran away, that's the strange thing, I had a phone call. It was your mother. I thought, at first, that's why you'd run away— because you knew where she was and had gone to see her. But, of course, that was impossible. She said she was in a detention centre. She didn't tell me much more. She just asked me to come and see her and to bring you with me. I didn't tell her you'd run away. I promised I'd bring you. And now I can.'

'When?' Amina asked. 'Can we go now?'

'Patience,' Aunt Victoria said. 'It takes time to arrange a visit. First you're coming home with me. A hot bath and a proper meal, that's what you need. Agreed?'

'What about James?' Amina said. 'And the police?'

'Don't worry about James,' Aunt Victoria said. 'I've given him a good talking to. And as far as the police are concerned, you're my niece and what happened was just a family quarrel.'

'I have to talk to Paul,' Amina said.

She ran over to where he was sitting and squatted beside him. 'I'm going back with Auntie Vickie,' she said.

'It's the best thing,' Paul said. 'Did she tell you where your mum is?'

'Yes,' Amina said. 'She told me everything.'

'Aren't you going to tell me?'

'It's too complicated now. Another time.'

They both stood up and looked at each other awkwardly.

'What about you?' Amina said. 'What will you do?'

'I'll be all right,' Paul said. 'Write to me. Write to me at the Crescent Moon. I'll give you the address.'

He wrote it down on a page from his exercise book and handed it to her. 'Let me know what happens,' he said.

She tore off a bit of paper and wrote down Aunt Victoria's address. 'I'll miss you,' she said.

'Jeepers creepers, me too,' he said.

She went to him and gave him a quick hug. Then she ran back to Aunt Victoria.

'Keep singing,' he shouted after her.

'OK. I'm ready,' Amina said.

8

Another journey begins

Dear Paul,

Here I am, back at Auntie Victoria's. We all had a good cry when I came home. Is it home? Well, I don't have to climb in through the back window so I suppose it is. I was worried that Cleo and Lawrence would be angry with me but they seemed really pleased to see me. I don't think James is though. He's just ignoring me but I don't care. Anyway, he's going away to camp soon with his friends.

Here's the big news. My mum is here in England in a detention centre. I didn't understand what that was when Auntie Vickie first told me. But I know now. It's a place where they lock up refugees. Auntie Vickie says it's not a prison and my mum hasn't done anything wrong. But I don't know why my mum has to be locked up and Auntie Vickie doesn't know either. Anyway, she's arranging for me to go with her to visit my mum soon. I can't really believe it. I'm going to see my mum!!! I don't know if I'll recognize her. I'm so nervous about it I can't sleep but I'm excited, too, cos I really want to see her. I want to know where I came from and what happened to her after she lost me. Well, she didn't exactly lose me. Anyway, it's complicated. I'll tell you about it one day.

How are you? Did you find somewhere to live? How is Leyla? How is the Crescent Moon? Are you still working there? I hope no one was hurt in that fight. I hope your guitar wasn't broken. Write to me and tell me what you're doing.

Your friend,
Amina

PS   Give my love to Leyla. I think of her a lot.
PPS   I'm singing with Cleo. We might form a group when we get a bit older.
PPPPPPS   I'M GOING TO SEE MY MUM!

Dear Jeepers Creepers,

It's great news that you'll soon be seeing your mum. I wish I could be there, too. You've got to tell me all about it, don't forget.

I went back to the Crescent Moon when I left you. It was a bit of a mess. The window was smashed and there was broken furniture and crockery all over the place. Mrs Onen has a cut on her forehead but I don't think anyone was hurt very much. From what Leyla said, the men who attacked the café came off worst. She said Mrs Onen hit one of them over the head with a frying pan and he ran off and the others ran away when the police came. I don't think the police caught any of them.

Anyway, it's all repaired now and the café's open again. I'm still working here. And guess what, I'm living here, too. Mrs Onen cleared the room upstairs with all the boxes in where I left my guitar. She gave me a mattress and even a sheet, a pillow, and a duvet. Real luxury. I have to pay rent out of my wages but I don't mind because I feel at home here. And I don't have far to walk to work, do I? When I thanked her, she said that's what we were put on this earth for—to help others who were in trouble. If that's true (is it?) lots of people don't know it. Especially those men who attacked the café.

I went back to our house to see if I could get some more of my stuff but I couldn't get in. The back window's well barricaded now. And someone's painted nasty slogans on the walls. I don't know why people want to do that.

I'm playing the guitar a lot but I've given up writing stories. I'm writing songs instead. The thing is, I need

*someone to sing them. If you and Cleo form a group,
can I join? (Only joking.)*

Leyla sends her love. Me too.

Paul

*PS   Maybe I'll come and visit you one day. Shall
I?*

PPS   I'M USING THE TOASTER!

Amina was glad to climb out of the car and
stretch her legs. It had been a long drive. She
looked up at the high wire fence with its rolls of
barbed wire on top. Behind the wire, she could
see dull red-brick buildings. It is a prison, she
thought to herself. She couldn't imagine why
her mother had been put in such a place. What
must it be like to live surrounded by fences
and barbed wire and not to be allowed
outside?

A guard opened the steel gate for visitors
and they went through into the reception area.
Two bored-looking guards were standing
behind the counter chatting. They wore crisp
white shirts and black trousers. Walkie-talkies
were attached to their black belts and badges
with their first names on were pinned to their
shirts. The guard whose badge said he was
Guy asked them who they were and who

they'd come to see. Aunt Victoria told him and he checked off their names on a list.

'Now then, miss,' he said to Amina. 'Stand over there and we'll take your photo.'

Amina did as she was asked in a kind of daze and then watched as Aunt Victoria also had her photo taken.

'I'm afraid I'll have to search your bag,' Guy told Aunt Victoria.

He rummaged through it, removing her chequebook, nail scissors, nail file, and car keys.

'You can't take those in with you,' he said.

Aunt Victoria looked amazed. 'Why not?' she asked.

'Rules,' Guy said and winked.

Aunt Victoria threw everything back in the bag and gave it to Guy. 'Might as well keep the bag here then,' she said.

'Fair enough. How about you, miss? What have you got in your pockets?'

'I haven't got any pockets,' Amina said. 'I haven't got anything.'

'What's this?' Guy said, pointing at her gold chain.

'I'm not taking that off,' Amina said.

'Sorry,' Guy said. 'It's the key. You'll have to leave it here.'

'No,' Amina said.

'You'll get it back when you leave, don't worry.'

'No,' Amina said.

'Look,' Aunt Victoria said. 'It's very important to her. She never takes it off. It's got her name on it. It's all she has from her childhood.'

'No keys,' Guy insisted. 'That's the rule.'

'I won't go in then,' Amina said tearfully.

'Have a heart,' Aunt Victoria said. 'She's going to see her mother. She hasn't seen her for seven years. Don't spoil it. Please.'

The guard looked doubtful. Then his face relaxed and he waved them through. 'OK,' he said. 'We'll bend the rules this once.'

A woman guard came in and frisked them before they were finally allowed through.

Amina's eyes were blazing. 'Why did they do that?' she said.

'Perhaps they thought we were trying to smuggle in machine guns,' Aunt Victoria laughed.

They walked across a yard to another steel gate which opened magically when they pressed the bell. Another guard, sitting in front of a computer, was waiting for them in the office. Amina peered at his name badge. It said Clive. He checked their names on the computer, made them sign the visitors' book, and gave them each a visitors' badge.

'Through there,' he said.

They walked into the visitors' room and sat down at one of the tables. There were other visitors there talking earnestly to refugees.

'Do you feel nervous?' Aunt Victoria asked.

'I don't know,' Amina said. 'I don't know what I feel. I'm numb. And I've got a tummy ache.'

'There'll be a toilet here,' Aunt Victoria said.

Amina shook her head. 'It's not that sort of tummy ache.'

They waited. The knot in Amina's stomach tightened. Just as she was wondering how much longer they would have to wait, a woman appeared at the end of the room and looked around uncertainly. She was small and slight, dressed simply in a long white blouse and white cotton trousers. Amina stood up and ran towards her, then stopped. The woman moved towards her slowly. They looked at each other. It seemed to Amina that she was looking at an older version of herself. The same olive skin, the same dark brown eyes, the same black hair and full mouth. She was, Amina thought, the most beautiful woman she'd ever seen.

'Mama,' Amina said.

The woman put her hand out to touch Amina's face with the tips of her fingers. 'Amina?'

The next moment, she wrapped her arms around her daughter and the tears began to flow. They held each other for a long time. Amina inhaled the warm fresh smell of her mother's skin and felt on her face her mother's salty tears mingling with her own. Then she became conscious of the people in the room staring at them. She pulled herself away and led her mother to where Aunt Victoria was sitting. Her mother kissed Aunt Victoria on both cheeks.

'Thank you,' she said.

They sat round the table, Amina's mother still clasping her daughter's hand.

'Well?' Aunt Victoria said. 'What do you think of her? Did you recognize her?'

'Certainly,' Amina's mother said. 'She is my child, my daughter. I have waited so long, so long for this moment. How can I tell you?'

Again tears began to trickle down her cheeks.

Why did you leave me then? Amina thought to herself. Why didn't you take me with you?

But what she said was, 'It's all right, Mum, it's all right.'

'I'm sorry. I must stop crying. It is silly.'

'Not at all,' Aunt Victoria said.

They sat there in silence, looking at each other.

'So many things to say,' Amina's mother said. 'Where to begin?'

'I think,' Aunt Victoria said, 'Amina would like you to tell her your story. Where you came from. How you came here. What happened to you when you left the hostel. Everything. I'd like to hear it, too.'

'I cannot tell you everything,' Amina's mother said. 'No one can. But I can tell you a story that begins at the almost beginning once upon a time more than fifty years ago. This is how the story was told to me. There is a village near Jerusalem in a country called Palestine. A family lives in the village in a beautiful stone house. It has been their home for generations. Mother, father, and two children, a girl aged ten and a boy aged eight. But their lives are about to change. People have come from the west with their pain and their suffering, Jews fleeing persecution. Now they have been given a country. Palestine is cut in two. The villagers do not understand. How can their land be given away? I remember my mother saying it was as if they did not exist, as if they had become invisible.

'Then comes fighting. Then comes war. One April day, in the pale sunshine, the soldiers arrive. They invade the village. They tell the villagers and the family to leave. "This is our home now," they say. "Our Promised Land. Go." For them the Promised Land. For us *al Nakba*, the catastrophe. So the family pack a few belongings and they leave. As they leave, they hear loud explosions. They turn, terrified, and see their house has gone. One after the other, the houses explode, crash to the ground. In the end, the village is nothing but a pile of rubble.'

'What was the name of the village?' Amina asked in a low voice.

'It was called Qalunya,' her mother answered. 'But you will not find it on the map.'

'It's on here, though, isn't it?' Amina said excitedly, pulling out the gold disc at the end of the chain.

'Yes,' her mother said. 'For the memory. For not forgetting. So the family leave, shocked and afraid. They join the long line of men, women, children, babies, donkeys, on the dusty road to nowhere. Refugees in their own land. The last thing they hear is the sound of a dog whining. The father carries a suitcase. The mother a bundle of clothes. The girl clutches a wooden box that her father has made. It contains the family jewellery. This is her future. Her jewellery. A soldier casts his eyes on the box and seizes it. She screams at him. It is as if her future is being taken away from her and there is nothing she can do.

'They walk for days, hungry, thirsty, exhausted. They cannot carry the suitcase any longer. They cannot carry the bundle of clothes any longer. The road is littered with suitcases, clothes, kitchen things, the belongings that the refugees can no longer carry. When they finally arrive at a place where there are no invaders, where they can be safe, they have nothing but the clothes they stand up in. And a key that the girl has kept, the key to the jewellery box. She keeps it for hope and for not forgetting.'

Amina looked down at the key on the end of her gold chain.

'Yes,' her mother said. 'That is the key. And that is the first part of this story. Do you want to hear more?'

Amina nodded.

'In their hearts,' Amina's mother said, 'they

hope to return to their own home. But in their heads, they know that this is impossible. There is nothing left for them to return to. So they try to make a new life where they are. It is hard at the beginning. The first winter is terrible. Their shelter is a tent. Food is scarce. Some days they have nothing to eat. Some days only bread. But they survive. They build a new stone house. The father works as a carpenter. The children go to school. Life begins again. The years pass. Now it is twenty years later. The girl has grown up. She has married a young man from the village, the son of the baker. They have a little baby girl.'

'Is that you?' Amina asked. 'Are you the baby girl?'

'Yes. I am two years old when war comes again. When invasion comes again. When the story begins all over again. The same story. The soldiers come. The land is occupied. The village is destroyed. Amwas. You will not find it now on the map. The family are divided. My grandparents say they will not leave. The young man, my uncle, also. They find shelter in a nearby village. My mother and father decide to leave, to find another country, another home. They take money and jewellery and they make a long journey.

'They travel through Jordan, Syria, and into Lebanon. They are taken with other refugees to a camp in the south of Lebanon. It is not what they wanted but they are tired and the baby is unwell. They decide to stay a little while. The little while stretches into years. There are people there helping the refugees. They come from many countries. Nurses, doctors, teachers. Some from England. That is how I learned English. I grew up there. I went to school there. I met Jamil, your father, there. We lived through more fighting, another invasion. My mother became ill. It was as if she was tired, too tired to live. I loved her very much. You were born there, a year after I married Jamil. You were named after my mother. Amina.

'But there was no peace. Sometimes there were shells. Sometimes bombs. People were being killed. The Israelis were occupying the south of the country. Jamil, your father, went to join the fighters who were trying to drive them out. They said he died a hero. I said I would rather have a live husband than a dead hero. My father said I should go, leave, find somewhere where there was peace. Somewhere I could live a normal life. He said he was too old to make any more journeys. I had some money. I sold my mother's jewellery. I wept with my father. And I left with my baby. Another journey begins. Do you remember anything, Amina?'

'No,' Amina said. 'Nothing.'

'Well, it doesn't matter. The journey is not important. All that matters is that at the journey's end, we came here, me and my child. It took a long time and all my money and nearly all my strength.'

She stopped and held Amina to her as if frightened of losing her again.

Aunt Victoria brushed away a tear. 'Such a sad story,' she said. 'What you must have gone through. And afterwards? What happened after the hostel?'

'I could see you were a good woman,' Amina's mother said. 'I knew you would look after my daughter. And I knew they would not let me stay. Could I tell them this story? No. They would send me away to I don't know where. So I made another journey. I met a friend who said he would help me and I made a journey north to Manchester. I found a job in a supermarket and rented a room. Better than nothing. I took an evening course in music. I've always loved singing. I got a better job in a bookshop. And every day I thought of you, Amina. Every day I wanted to come and find you and take you back with me. But I was afraid. I was illegal, after all. And what could I give you? Could I spoil the good life you were having? Take you away from this family, this house, your friends, your school? So I said I will wait until I have a better life, a home—'

'You should have come,' Amina almost shouted. 'You should have come and fetched me.'

'I'm sorry,' her mother said. 'I'm sorry. I did what I thought was best for you.'

'How come you're here?' Aunt Victoria asked. 'What happened?'

'I had a friend. He *was* a friend. Stupidly, I trusted him. Then he was a not friend. And this not friend told the police I was illegal.'

'Will they let you out? What's going to happen to you?'

'I have a lawyer,' Amina's mother said. 'A good lawyer, I think. He is asking for exceptional leave to remain.'

'What's that mean?' asked Amina.

'Then I'll be allowed to stay,' her mother said. 'He says I have a good case because I've been in the country so long and I have a daughter who's been brought up here.'

'We'll keep our fingers crossed,' Aunt Victoria said. 'Is it awful here? Isn't it like being in prison?'

'It's bad enough,' Amina's mother said. 'Every day the same. The same awful food. The same hallways. Uniforms watching you. Voices shouting at you. And rules. Always rules.' She sighed. 'I'm sorry, I think I must go now.'

They all stood up. Amina hugged her mother hard.

'See you soon, Mum,' she said.

'See you soon,' her mother said.

'Only,' Amina said, 'I'm still not sure where I come from. Where I belong.'

'You have two countries,' her mother said. 'Like you have two mothers. England and Palestine.'

'Will we ever go back to Palestine?'

Her mother raised her hands, palms upwards to the heavens. 'I don't know. Who knows? Maybe. One day. *Insh'Allah*. God willing.'

9

'Are we going to let them do it?'

Three weeks later, she was back in the car park outside the detention centre. They were all there. Aunt Victoria was beside her and Leyla behind her. She could see Mama Luminita sitting in a wheelchair surrounded by her children. The sun shone down on the flags and the balloons and the placards saying CLOSE HARMFORTH DETEN-TION CENTRE and HANDS OFF OUR FRIENDS. Paul was on the platform playing his guitar with an expression of intense concentration on his face. He was accompanying a tall girl who was singing a song about refugees.

Amina felt a pang of jealousy. Why wasn't

she on the platform singing? She could sing as well as that girl, anyway.

A line of policemen stood between the demonstrators and the detention centre, ready to intercept anyone who tried to attack the fence. At the end of the line, Amina spotted Redface and his friend. They were still wearing their dark blue suits despite the summer heat. Redface had a camera and was taking photos of the demonstrators. Amina turned to Leyla and pointed them out.

'Don't worry,' Leyla said. 'They won't do anything. They wouldn't dare.'

Applause greeted the end of the song. Paul stumbled off the platform clutching his guitar and pushed his way towards them. His face was flushed.

'How did it sound?' he said.

'Bravo!' Leyla said.

Amina smiled. 'You were good,' she said.

A man climbed onto the platform and began speaking into the microphone. 'Isn't that place a disgrace?' he said, waving his hand at the barbed wire fence and the red-brick buildings beyond.

'Yes!' came back the shouted reply from the crowd.

'They come to this country,' he went on,

'fleeing from torture, from hunger, from persecution, fleeing for their lives. And then they're treated like animals. Locked up like criminals.'

'What's happening with your mum?' Paul asked.

'Didn't you get my letter?' Amina said. 'I wrote to you everything she told me.'

'Yes,' Paul said. 'But are they letting her out?'

'I don't know yet,' Amina said.

'So we don't know the end of the story.'

'No,' Amina said.

Suddenly she heard her name being called. Voices were calling her. 'Amina. Amina. Where are you?'

'They want you on the platform,' Leyla whispered.

'What for?'

'Go on,' Aunt Victoria said. 'It'll help your mum.'

'Come up here, Amina,' the man on the platform said. 'Don't be shy.'

Amina felt herself being propelled towards the front of the crowd and onto the platform.

'This is Amina,' the man said. 'Her mother's locked up in the detention centre.'

'Shame!' someone shouted.

'Her mother could tell you a story that would break your heart. A story of endless war, pain, loss, and suffering. Then seven years ago, she came to this country with her baby girl and made a new life. Now all she wants is to be left in peace so she can make a home for herself and this lovely daughter of hers. Is that a crime?'

'No!' roared the crowd.

'But they say she's illegal. They lock her up. They threaten to deport her, to send her back. Back where? Back to suffering. Back to war. Back to hunger. Is that fair? Is that humane? Is that the act of a civilized country?'

'No!' roared the crowd.

'So are we going to let them do it?' the speaker said. 'Are we?'

Amina saw in the dazzling sunlight the faces of the crowd ready to respond, saw the balloons and the flags and the placards, saw Redface with his camera pointing towards her, saw Paul and Leyla and Aunt Victoria smiling up at her, and in one frozen flash of a moment, she felt herself soaring out of her body up into the blue sky and she was a brown bird, high above the earth, and her mother was a rainbow bird beside her and together they were flying, flying homeward to a place called nowhere . . .